A Shilling on the Bar

Hettie Ashwin

*To Sue
enjoy
Hettie*

Published by Slipperygrip

Copyright © Hettie Ashwin

All rights reserved

The moral right of the author has been asserted.

This book is sold subject to the condition that it shall not, by way of trade or otherwise, be lent, re-sold, hired out, or otherwise circulated without the author's proper consent in any form other than that in which it is published and without a similar condition including this condition being imposed on the subsequent purchaser.

ISBN 13: 978-1493769124

www.slipperygripcolumn.blogspot.com

www.hettieashwin.blogspot.com

Plate I

The photograph I held showed a rather fine fellow. His crowning feature was a large moustache expertly groomed. His clothes and his piercing eyes all spoke of one who commanded attention. The signature on the back of the photograph read,

Trododniak Weatherness.

If this was by his own hand he was a master of elegant penmanship. The casual even stokes showed someone who had not only skill, but execution. I once again looked at the likeness, then turned my attention to the papers which were accompanying the photograph in an old box. They were in no particular order but were bound by a ribbon of the legal variety.

I opened the bundle and removed a protective sheet of paper to reveal the title.

A Shilling on the Bar.

Collected Stories by

T. Weatherness.

Archer Frankston

Rufus Mcfadden

Erik Van Bootman

Boy

Martin Swinburne

Lionel Arkwright

Seymour Ham

Miss Willmott and Mr Crick

Edward Addison

Dolly & Harold Lancome

Flora Rhinehart

Pat

Albert Barrett & Friend

Lola & Reverend Stanley Pinks

Hal & Gloria Wafflebach

Bruno Cavello

Here I began to read.

Plate II

Archer Frankston

My train pulled out of the Roma street station and I settled in for the overnight journey. I had given myself three days to make my way to Cairns for the start of my annual circuit in Far North Queensland as a travelling Magistrate. I bustled about stowing my one bag and getting settled when I spied my cabin companion watching my every move with a serious study. He was a very elderly gentleman, bent over and with a lifetime of experience in his face. I introduced myself and sat down to read a book I had purchased, but his constant stare was un-nerving and so I enquired as to his journey, and after a few civil pleasantries regarding the troops we were carrying and their final destination passed between us, I settled back in my seat.

My companion seeing I was less inclined to read asked if I was up for a story. I put my book down and nodded in the affirmative and this was how he began.

It was with a source of pride that Archer Frankston remained a bachelor. A man of wealth and reasonable education his only set back a particularly skewed top lip which could go from smile to snarl as quick as the wind changed. There had been women in Archer's life. Women who seduced him. Women who pandered to his ego, but Mr. Frankston remained the pillar of strength against their feminine wiles. Mr Frankston was a man who seemed to demand his way in life and none dare say no.

His father beat him into obedience and the model of discipline embedded itself into Archer to be repeated at boarding school and later at university. Peers of the time would later describe Master Frankston as the one who held the stick, but also the carrot. That carrot was money. Archer's largess upon his friends became as legendary as his whippings and Archer knew how to use both to his advantage.

His first encounter with the opposite sex began with his mother. Mrs. Frankston was to Archer about as close to heaven as he could get. He adored his mother and none could compare to her kindness, her unwavering adoration of her son and her beauty. There was something a little unnerving about the mother/son relationship and when Audrey Frankston died, Archer still a young lad, took his adoration to a higher level and beatified his love on the mantle-piece in the front parlour. Although, Archer in his misguided youth, also hated his mother for leaving him in the hands of his less than forgiving father.

Glenda Flack was an angel in Archer's eyes, but try as she might she was a sad reflection of the one true love in Archer's life. They met at the university prom, Glenda studying the Arts and Archer studying Glenda. She was a petite girl of refinement with a swathe of blonde hair swept up into an elaborate coiffure. At nineteen years of age Glenda had badgered her father to support her at university, one of the few women in the class in an age when women and enlightenment were not happy bedfellows. Her strident bearing, her forthright views and her pouting cherry red lips ensured Glenda had many admirers. For a young man who was accustomed to having his own way Archer pursued Miss Flack with a devotion his tutors wished he might reserve for his studies. Her stubbornness to oblige only fuelled his desire. Archer relished the game of chase, practicing the art of seduction until the day Glenda capitulated in a whirlwind of roses and fanciful dreams.

The tryst between Glenda and Archer was as violent as it was swift. For a young man who was bred on hard discipline and little else, Archer could not see the feminine point of view. His vision was clouded with power and lust. Glenda was no match for the predator and Archer left her a broken woman, her dreams shattered, her future uncertain. It was no surprise when Miss Flack disappeared from the campus, her friends bound to never mention the incident that led to her confinement at a distant relative's country estate. Archer oblivious to the outcome of his boorish behaviour, cultivated his sycophants, his fops and his friends, espousing his views on women and education, women and love and women and sex, so much so that he missed completely the small notice in the paper regarding the untimely demise of Miss Flack in unfortunate circumstances. What those circumstances were remained within the family.

Here my elderly companion knocked out his pipe on the heating system and replenished the small delicate bowl. I wondered as to the depth of knowledge this man had of his story, and why he felt compelled to tell it. He was a master of the telling and I knew I was almost completely under his spell. But, he had a way of studying my reactions to his tale that might make any man uneasy and I felt quite obliged to look away and watch the passing parade of hills in the distance as the train slowed for the tunnels to come. His pipe leapt into life and once again he grabbed my attention.

After university Archer slid into the family business of importing. His father, a firm believer in working your way up, required his son to learn the ropes and so Archer's first days at Frankston Importers was on the docks. It was in this rough environment Archer learnt what life had to offer if you had the knuckles and bluff. He fell into the camaraderie of the workers and earned a scar or two along the way. His father, rather than celebrating his son's success to engage the lower working classes, berated him for fraternizing. There is a line between management and workers Archer was told at the sharp end of a walking stick. That was the last time his father had the opportunity to assault him, because Archer lashed out in a fit of righteousness and the founder of Frankston Imports clutched his chest and fell down dead.

As the heir to the business Archer was in an enviable position. His accountant said imports were a licence to print money, but Archer saw it as a licence to spend. He didn't deny himself or his brigade of friends, and as his generosity grew so did his reputation. A reputation built on greed, extravagance, violence and lust.

The word lust was thrown at me and I dutifully winced. As much as my book looked a good option to this storyteller's grandiose gestures, I remained intrigued and listened attentively.

Trixie Smith was a woman who enjoyed an extravagant lifestyle on the purse of others and it was money that brought them together, desire that kept them in each other's company and lust that rent them asunder. They met in less than salubrious surroundings and consummated their hedonistic relationship in squalid lust. Trixie had had experience with men like Archer, but even she was a little frightened at his bastardry. If it wasn't for the money she might have walked away, but she didn't and it seemed to Archer, Trixie was the whipping boy he had always craved. Their relationship continued in fits and starts. Archer entertaining the idea of polite society, but always drawn back to Trixie and her accommodating ways, until one night he saw fear in her eyes as his fingers clutched ever tighter around her neck and she eventually slumped to the bed, dead.

Some men pay for their sins and then there are men like Archer who pay others for their sins. He called in his friends, reminding them of their obligations and Mr. Frankston was playing golf with friends at the time of Miss Smith's demise. He had only met the waif for philanthropic purposes and had no further interest in the story. It was a closed chapter in Archer Frankston's life, but less of a salutary lesson.

It seemed to those close to Archer he had a charmed life. While others were trying to earn a living and provide for wife and family, Frankston was living high. But if they had delved a little deeper than the champagne and various clubs, the outlook might have been different and they would thank providence for their mundane existence. Archer's mind was in a maelstrom of torment and he deceived himself with ill conceived platitudes and righteous lies, while he trod the path of servitude in Hades.

After Trixie there was a lust for life at the edge. He would tramp the inner slums looking for life's less fortunate and beguile them into sordid acts and then toss them aside with no more care than to kick a stray cat. The thrill of power over another's very life was like an opiate and Archer was addicted. It was only a matter of time before his luck would run out which made the addiction even more exciting. That is until he saw Netti Bromley.

Netti was from the London Bromleys who owned most of the docks on the east side. At twenty one Netti stood to inherit a fortune, but it was her beauty that suitors admired. With cascading black hair that framed a pale almost alabaster face with dark eyes, eyes that held a fanciful mystery of a Spanish ancestor and lips that beckoned with every smile, Nettie was almost too good to be true, or so Archer thought the moment he set his eyes on her. It seemed his life hadn't existed until he saw Netti and so with one smitten look he swept away the sourness, the bitter taste that had been his past and replaced it with a love for Netti Bromley.

All his cunning up 'till now had been mere trifles as he campaigned for an introduction and possibly a relationship. His chance came with a banquet for captains of industry hosted by those at the top of the financial ladder, including the Bromleys. Nettie was standing in the reception line next to her father in a gown of emerald green which clinched at the waist and gave a tantalizing lift to her delicate bust. Archer stood off to one side and watched as she greeted the guests while trying to keep one stray hair from falling out of place. He knew what to do and so walked over to the wall flowers sitting by the punch bowl and picked the plainest girl from the expectant bunch. It was a simple matter of a short promenade around the room and an indecent whisper in the girl's ear which elicited a blush and Archer had his prize and then, without so much as a bow, he cast the girl aside. Now with ammunition he waited in line to be received by Sir Bromley and his daughter. Archer bowed just enough and Netti took his hand as he slipped the purloined hair pin in hers. She looked at the pin then laughed and excused herself, turned her back and fixed the wayward strand of hair. It was a small matter to give her his card and retreat. He didn't stay for the dinner preferring to let Netti think on her gallant saviour and want to see him again. It was a game he had played before and he was sure of his tactics.

It only took two days and Miss Bromley wrote a short note inviting Mr. Frankston to a convivial afternoon tea with a short apology for not getting in touch sooner. Archer felt like a winner. And to celebrate he let himself be seduced into one last foray into the dark side, promising himself this would be the last and never again might the thrill of absolute power fire his black heart. It was a promise that would be hard to keep.

A knock at the door startled me and trying to recover my dignity I bade the guard enter. He was calling for lunch and told us we had just over an hour to eat in the dining car. My companion smiled and in a gesture of generosity asked for my company at his expense. I politely refused his offer, but even in his twilight years his insistence reminded me of a man who wasn't used to a refusal and so I acquiesce with the proviso I reciprocate with dinner. It was a hard won deal. We walked along the train stopping now and again to let other passengers pass and for him to catch his breath and presently arrived to the smells of a delicious menu. After our order had been taken my dining companion continued as we were served our wine.

The ritual of a night on the town for Archer started with a good meal. He would sup at one of the many chop houses in the city and then move on to an ale house. It would be well into the night before he finished his drinking and left the lively pub for the chill of the dark streets. Archer knew where to go and as he walked the alleyways and lanes around the dock, his desire strengthened to become an insatiable ache for fulfilment. Women who live in the dockland slums have little in the way of morals and can be generous with their bodies for the right customer and the right price. Archer recognised the greed in those who would satisfy his need and it wasn't long on that cold August evening before he found his mark. Lilly Magill thought she was on a winner that night with her customer proffering more money than she could make in a month. It was a done deal as she wrapped her cloak around her thinly covered bones and bade Archer to follow her to the warmth of her one room at the back of a bakery. She turned just once under the street lamp to see Archer's piercing stare and his top lip curling into a sneer and for a quick moment she might have had second thoughts, before she walked for the last time to her lodgings on Fishnet lane. Lilly Magill died without dignity and the most one could say was that death, when it did come that winter night, might have been a blessing. She was without family, therefore no one cried for justice, no one called for vengeance and she was buried as the unknown are forgotten.

Our meals arrived and I had lost my appetite.

"I can see you are a sensitive soul and my story has touched your heart," my companion said. I admitted I was shaken by the casual way he described poor Lilly's death. It seemed to me he had an intimacy with the story that belied the third person narration. Then he told me something that put his telling into perspective.

"I was a man of the faith, a servant of God and I pray every day for their souls. All of them."

"Was?" I asked. He nodded,

"Sometimes our calling can be a curse as well as a blessing. One has to forgive oneself before one can forgive others."

I pushed my vegetables around my plate and once again studied the scenery. He began to eat and presently I followed his lead, every mouthful a struggle as I ruminated over a life that seemed too close to the devil to be true, and a priest who seemed compelled to tell it. When our dessert arrived he continued and I once again fell under his spell.

Archer Frankston felt relief that night. He had made a pact with himself or with the better side of his nature and he meant to keep it. He stepped into the night, leaving Lilly and the devil behind and with a spring in his step walked to the main thoroughfare thinking of Netti and only Netti.

That first afternoon tea turned into a weekly event, Archer excelling in gracious behaviour, good manners, good breeding and expensive gifts. Netti, although flattered, was young and apt to make decisions on small fripperies and could not get used to Archer's lip. She unsuccessfully tried to distance herself from Archer, but Archer ingratiated himself to her father and his presence in the house was almost a given. It was around the three month mark when Archer, for all his fine ways, demanded a more intimate relationship from Netti and was rebuked. A kiss from such a lip was the last thing on Netti's mind and she made it clear to Archer that his presence in the house was now unwelcome.

A personal rebuff from the object of his desire was a cruel twist to his ego and Archer raged against the injustice. His mother had treasured his hair lip, saying he was kissed by the angels as a baby. His friends refused to acknowledge his disability, and he might have forgotten his impediment except for Netti's cruel remarks. To be rejected was a feeling that demanded retribution and although he had promised himself, his need was great, the desire all consuming. In his arrogance he presumed Netti needed to be taught a lesson and he would be the one to teach it. But the Bromley's were a class above those of the docklands and what passed in one quarter would not in another and so Archer shelved his vengeful feelings for Netti and took his anger elsewhere, Netti never realising how close she came to meeting the devil's own envoy. Maeve O'Donnell met the devil on that night when the new moon hid behind a bank of clouds. Maeve needed the money and Archer seemed a swanky gent willing to give it up. Their encounter was swift and vicious as Archer broke his promise and lay waste a pitiful life. His reasoning was as twisted as his soul as he cajoled himself to believe that Maeve was the last. His Netti was young and impressionable and she would soon see the error of her judgement Archer thought. He would try again.

There were gifts, flowers, tickets to the theatre and more as Archer wooed Netti with his vast fortune behind him. Netti was flattered and though she had spurned Archer once she enjoyed the game safe in the knowledge that they both knew the rules. Archer was single minded in his quest for the young girl, his lust for her as great as his desire for acceptance. Several times Netti extended the boundaries and teased Archer with a clandestine kiss or held his arm on a Sunday promenade, and gave Archer a hope that was far beyond the reality. It was a dangerous game Netti played while innocent of the true metal of Archer Frankston.

A dangerous game indeed, the old man stressed.

We finished with coffee and replete made our way back to the confines of the carriage. I was on edge now wanting to continue and wasted no time in sitting down and looking expectant. My companion drew out the moment by packing his pipe and then spying my face full of hope, he smiled and continued.

There came a time in the relationship when Archer thought he was advanced enough in Netti's affections to ask for a formal undertaking. He had purged himself of his habits, though not without difficulty, and felt sufficiently cleansed by his efforts. So with his heart on his sleeve he went to see Sir

Bromley. He had cultivated Sir Bromley as much as his daughter and felt some satisfaction that the father might persuade the daughter if she was dithering at all. What he didn't know was that as the way of young ladies, they are will 'o' wisps in matters of the heart and Netti had fallen for another, an officer of the Royal Regiment, while still dallying with Archer. It was an audience of less than five minutes, but in that time Archer went from winner to loser and for all his abstinence, his black heart seethed.

"She never wants to see you again Mr Frankston," Sir Bromley said adding, "sorry," when he saw Archer's expression of dismay and confusion. Archer left the Bromley household a possessed man and it would be well into the early hours of the morning before his anger was quelled and another life snuffed out, like the gas lamps at sunrise. Archer returned to his house and fell into morbid turbidity, his promise broken once again.

In the month Archer locked himself away from the world the authorities, the papers and public remained ignorant of the whereabouts of The Dockland Choker, a populist moniker for the perpetrator of the ghastly murders at the dockside. Archer relished his notoriety while abhorring his need to fuel it, with only his psychotic mind finding logic in his heinous deeds. Then in his addictive state he made a plan. He began to stalk young Netti, furtively, surreptitiously with malicious intent. Her movements, her social engagements, her outings became Archer's itinerary. He would fuel his contempt for women with power over the weaker sex. His journeys to the docks became more frequent, his misogynist thirsts for command unquenchable. There was no stopping his manic behaviour as he ramped up his anger for the one final showdown.

That showdown came one spring morning with the announcement of the marriage of Netti Bromley to Capt'n Hartley Ashcroft of the Queens Regiment. Archer read the social column and knew his time had come. The cathedral was a grand backdrop for the society wedding, and a grand setting for his final act.

That Saturday Archer had a plan. He dressed immaculately, ate heartily and then with deliberate actions went to his bureau and retrieved his pistol. Archer had a fascination with his gun. The Browning was purchased as a precursor to his participation in the war, but as the owner of a seconded supply ship his efforts were needed far from the killing fields, and although Archer decried his war effort, he relished his need for the weapon and the absolute power it contained. He loaded just one shot and put the weapon in his jacket pocket. As he stepped out into the bright crisp morning, Archer felt he had a purpose, a power he had never felt before. He made his way to the cathedral and presented himself at the door just as the verger opened them for the morning. Archer stepped inside and breathed deeply. Men like Archer have a mindset that applauds their choices in life. They rationalise their sins and their only judge is their ego. But there is a higher court. One that can see through a man's debasements and as Archer stood on the threshold of

God's house his heart was rent with God's arrow. All his sins crowded his mind and as he fell to his knees, his wayward soul cried out for forgiveness. While he knelt a gentle hand pressed on his shoulder and he looked up to see a priest. No words were necessary as Archer stood and followed the messenger of God to the chapel of remembrance in the eastern transept. It was here Archer began his journey of forgiveness.

"You may think a man cannot change in an instant," my companion said looking right at me and he was right. I had my doubts. "But I have seen it, and I believe it can happen," he said.

Archer relived his past with that priest, but as he talked and wept and pleaded he began to realise only God could absolve him.

It was to be the wedding of the year so the society pages boasted. Netti Bromley had a gown that was designed for the season and as she pulled up her train to step into her carriage none could be happier. It was a short trip to the cathedral and there her groom would be waiting and their future could be nothing but bright.

Archer, relieved of his burden fell asleep and woke up to guests filling the great hall. He adjusted his jacket and it was then he felt the lump that was his pistol and his murderous intent flooded his mind and a battle raged within; good versus evil. He sat still and tried to pray but no thoughts would come, no words of comfort, nothing from God, and he felt cheated. Mendelssohn's wedding march was heralding the bride's entrance and Archer stood with the congregation.

    Netti was smiling holding her father's arm as she looked ahead to the alter and the Captain. Archer watched her and his top lip began to pucker, a tightening of his muscle, a sneer emerging as his heart beat with vengeance. She was almost at the altar when Archer thrust his way to the aisle and strode purposefully towards the couple. He broke into a trot as the bridesmaids moved to one side and the couple knelt for the blessing. Then, when he reached Sir Bromley he pulled his gun from his pocket. Sir Bromley reacted with a horrified gasp and Netti turned to see Archer raise the weapon to take aim at her breast. She screamed in terror, her voice reaching the lofty heights of the cupola and stood to rush to her father's side when Captain Ashcroft in an act of bravery, lunged for the Browning, and it was then, in that instant, the priest looked Archer in the eye and Archer stopped, turned the gun on himself and pulled the trigger.

    I let out a gasp. It was as unexpected as it was swift and my pulse was beating fast. Gradually, sitting in silence, I regained my composure. I watched while my travelling companion knocked the stem of his pipe on his teeth and looked out the window at the darkening vista as dusk enveloped the fields and farms. He closed his eyes and I ruminated on his involvement so long ago. As the cabin lights came on I knew I didn't need to know. The story was enough.

Plate III

Rufus McFadden

    The roads around Eidesvold can be described as basic. They were cut from the scrub once and never visited again. Ruts, holes and ditches are the norm and after a big wet season they can disappear altogether. I had the loan of a car in the hope of getting to my destination a little quicker, but it was a false hope.
    I had been waiting three days for a spare part and almost given up of ever leaving Eidesvold. The town was built on cattle, but the few souls that inhabited the town now, seemed to me, to live on fresh air. There were empty shelves in the stores and the garage that boasted car maintenance and repairs didn't carry anything useful at all. The mechanic, Mr Cooper, assured me for the umpteenth time that the vital part

was on its way. He was certain of it. I had my doubts and let him know. We looked at the car jacked up over a pit and he scratched his chin.

Used to be we could get anything and everything. It wasn't always like this, he began. The road to town was the only road and it was well used as people came here looking for a little bit o' land. We had gold here in the way of pasture. There's still some land around for those that want to work for it. Anyways, the town had a shop, post office and all the things people needed to live, but still, it was the odd things that were missing. Shoe polish, garden hoe, rubberbands, red ribbons, glue. All the little things that make life a bit more bearable. So we had Rufus McFadden.

Was he Scottish? I said
Dunno. Maybe.

Anyway Rufus used to swing by here once or twice a year, maybe more I can't remember exactly. Cooper scratched his head and thought for a bit. Maybe three times, it's hard to say. Anyways, he was a little fella. Sort of not quite finished growing, if you know what I mean. He had a keen eye for a bargain and an even keener eye for money. I tell ya nothing could be put past McFadden. They said he counted his money every night and slept with a wad under his pillow. They said he was rich. He always had a nice watch on a chain and it was a gold chain. Perhaps he was rich. Cooper thought on the proposition for a bit and I could imagine the cogs turning in his mind as he thought it over. Anyways, he made a decent living off the folks. He was one of those travelling blokes that drive around the country selling things. Mind you, I was only a tyke when he was around but I still remember the truck. An old Albion truck. 32 Break horse power.

Remember the badge? Cooper asked. Sure as the sunrise. It was one of those trucks the Arnotts Biscuits Company used.
I smiled, remembering the logo of the parrot and it brought back fond memories for me. Cooper hitched his trousers, spat on the ground and went on.

Don't ask me where he got it from, but he had it fitted out to take his wares. Shelves, boxes, and little drawers, that sort of thing. He had the truck painted in red and put his name on the side. And he had a bell. One of those fireman bells. Can you imagine the excitement as a lad when we'd hear that bell. 'Cause Rufus McFadden had everything. Or so it seemed to me.
My family used to live on the west side of town and Mcfadden would always come from the west, so we were the first stop. We had first dibs on what he had to offer. But the thing was, you never quite knew when he was coming. He'd just turn up and ring that bell. It was sort of exciting not knowing. One day you'd be coming home from school and not thinking of much besides getting home and then you'd hear that bell. I tell you, we used to run like the wind to catch up with the truck. It felt like Christmas.

Cooper picked his teeth with a screwdriver and thought for a bit.

I don't recollect him coming for Christmas. Maybe once or twice.

Well, he'd stop the truck on our street and wait. My mates and I would be going over the truck, looking at the wheels, asking questions about the engine, that sort of thing. Annoying him something chronic, but he never seemed to mind. If you stayed around long enough he just might give you something. A thick rubber for your slingshot, a box of matches, a bit of string. All good things to a small lad.

The thought of childhood made me smile.
Boys will be boys, I said.

Mcfadden had a soft spot for kids I reckon. I don't know if he was married. Probably not 'cause he was always travelling. Anyways, we all liked him. Everyone liked him, well when I say everyone, I mean our mothers and the ladies of the town. They all liked him too. The ladies would come out and shoo the kids away and then Mcfadden would start opening his boxes and things.

If Mrs Drysdale wanted ribbon, he had it. If Molly Smith needed a cooking pot, Mcfadden knew just what sort and if Mrs Pelham was looking for a picture frame for a photograph, Rufus could put his hand on the size and style. It was like that. Whatever a lady wanted, he had it. He just sort of knew what you wanted, even before you did. I needed a puncture repair kit for my bicycle tyre once and blow me down if Mcfadden didn't have it. He was canny like that. Don't ask me how he kept it all on that truck, but it was a treasure trove.

The best part of Mcfadden coming to town was that he would let us sit in the truck and mind it while he did his business. My mother always needed something or other and then Mcfadden would be shown into the house and asked his opinion. Curtain material, mats, tea cups, hair brushes, anything. He'd be inside giving his opinion on things and then my mother would buy something. Sometimes he was such a good salesman, she'd buy something we already had. I tell you there were a lot of tablecloths in our house.

Then he'd move on to the next house and the next. Once, when I was about 8, I guess, he let me drive the truck down the street to Mrs Macdonalds. It was a good half a mile. I tell you, that set my heart on a truck when I was old enough. All I wanted to be was just like Mcfadden. I asked my mother to change my name to Rufus. Of course she refused, but I used to sign my name Rufus all the same. He seemed about the most magical thing that ever happened in Eidesvold.

Cooper picked up a wrench and then thought the better of it and picked up a scrap of wood and began to clean his fingernails. I looked on thinking he was hopeful as the grease had built up over a lifetime.

Well, when he was done, Rufus would drive out of town and it seemed to me just disappear in a cloud of dust. I don't know where he went, or where he came from and it didn't really matter. What mattered was when he was in town. As I grew a bit he would let me drive the truck right through the town, stopping at all the houses along the way. He'd let a couple of other mates drive too, and then he'd pay us. It was the first shilling I made looking after the truck while he showed Mrs Joyce his new dressing table sets. You can see why we liked him.

I nodded.

I guess it was just around that time that he stopped coming. We had a new shop in town. One of those emporium types. They would bring all the goods in by truck, a fleet of Chevrolets. One tonners I think. Anyways, the store seemed to carry everything. Everything that Mcfadden carried. I guess he couldn't compete with that. A lot of the old ways die out eventually. The modern world catches up with even the smallest town. The emporium did well for a while, but there just wasn't the demand for all their finery. My mother said that she missed the personal touch. You know, the individual attention that Mcfadden could provide. I certainly missed the bell.

The new store was down the street, near the hotel. Burnt down a while back. Right to the ground and took the bank with it. They didn't rebuild. No sense in flogging a dead horse. There was talk of an insurance job, but I don't know anything about that. Mind you, you wonder, don't you?

Cooper studied his boots then sighed.
Did Mcfadden come back after that? I asked.

Not then. Some said he went somewhere out west where they don't have fancy shops. Anyways, we couldn't afford all the fancy stuff as the twins came along.

Your siblings?
Yeah. Bob and Joe. Cooper looked at the dirty calendar on the wall and frowned.

So it must have been around a year after they arrived that Mcfadden suddenly came into town. We'd almost forgotten that bell by then. I can tell you there was a great fuss. It was like he was royalty or something. You never seen so many women crowding around that Albion truck. I recollect it was a school day 'cause I couldn't drive, but it looked like he would be busy all day with the ladies.

Well he did his rounds that day and then we saw him regular after that. Every month he'd drive into town still selling things women need. All the fancy stuff they can't live without. My mother must have saved, 'cause she always had Mcfadden giving his opinion on this or that. I was mostly at school, but sometimes he'd leave a trinket for me. A pen knife, a book on animal tracks, a tortoise shell comb. He was good like that. The twins didn't miss out either. A pop gun, a tin car, a whistle. I guess my mother was one of his best customers.

I looked at Cooper and wondered why he didn't think too hard on the story he was telling. It seemed obvious to me. He picked up a rag and wiped the back of his neck, either wiping grease on or off, it was a moot point, and took up the story.

I guess I was about 10 when he stopped coming altogether. Of course the ladies in the town weren't happy. They had to send away for the things they needed and it just wasn't the same. You can't discuss things with a catalogue. We had a bus service start around that time and my mother would take us into town, Mundubbera, but it wasn't a patch on Rufus. I don't think he will be forgotten in Eidesvold. So many kids grew up with him and that bell.

Cooper wiped his nose on his sleeve and stood with his hands in his pockets.

I must have been around 20 when one day this bloke comes into the garage. I didn't own it then, but was working my trade. So this bloke is waiting for an oil change and we get to talking. Turns out Mcfadden used to come to his town too. Same thing. He said he knew of about four other towns around the area. It was the first I had heard of Mcfadden for years and then this bloke says Mcfadden gave the game away.
Gave the game away? I asked. Yeah. He sold the Albion. I would have like to own that truck. It was always in good condition. Rufus looked after it. Regular services, good brakes and tyres. So I'm talking to this fella and he says he knows where Mcfadden is living. Not that I wanted to see the old man or anything, but I was kinda curious. I told my mother about the

conversation and she said she'd like to know where he was too. So I decided to go looking.

You know when you get an idea in your head and it won't let go. Well I stewed on that idea for almost a year. And then I went.

Where? I said.

Everywhere.

And did you find him?

Well...Cooper perched on the bench.

I didn't exactly find him. I found where he had been though.

What do you mean? I asked.

Well..., Cooper picked up a hammer and weighed it up in his hands. Mcfadden might not have been the best looking bloke around, but you couldn't miss him on account of his red hair.

Ah, I said.

Yeah. I guess he knew just what women want.

Cooper put down the hammer and picked up a bent spring and began to worry it straight.

So when I was looking I heard he had gone bush. Right out in the scrub. Anyways, I didn't say anything to my mum. It's not the kinda thing you can talk about. So, it was a few years later when this fella drives into the garage. I owned it by then. It must have been about eight years or so when I think about it. I was married and coming up to having my first.

First?

A boy, Rodney. Well a Ford drives up and this carrot top gets out. He's my age and we sort of hit it off. William was his name. From Biloela. He needed a radiator hose. Those hoses are all different. I had several, but not the one he needed. We get to talking and I say that his hose will be a day away and things weren't always like this and I mention Mcfadden. Anyways, William says he knew of Mcfadden and heard from a bloke in Mount Isa that Mcfadden had been seen in the bush with some aboriginals. Way out west.

You ever been West Mr Weatherness? Cooper asked me.
Yes several times.
Not much there is there?
Not much. I said.
Anyways, William says this bloke said there was a mob of aboriginals out in the middle of nowhere and they all had red hair. Can you imagine that?
Really.
Yeah.
Cooper hopped down from the bench and walked to the doorway. He stood with his hands in his overall pockets and looked out to the road.
It's a pity Mcfadden wasn't here. I bet he would have that part you need. Cooper turned and looked at me, the sun catching his shock of red hair.
I guess it will be here any day now, he said.

Plate IV

Erik Van Bootman.

A port town is different from any other town. The population is itinerant, the laws are those of the sea and there are usually more pubs per square mile than you can visit in a week.

I was looking for a place to eat in Gladstone. Not a fancy restaurant, but somewhere with a homely feel and a dinner of meat and three vegetables. I was pointed in the right direction by a policeman and turned the corner to see the Slipway Arms.

It looked a fair place with a blackboard pinned to the wall advertising the tasty fare.

It was dark and cool as I walked up to the bar and ordered my roast of the day and a drink. The sun refused to penetrate into the front bar as if stepping over the threshold was forbidden and so the gloom made the décor look almost inviting.

The place was near empty for a lunch time and I fleeting wondered if I had made a mistake with my choice, but gradually the place thickened with hungry people and thirsty drinkers until it was very nearly standing room only at 12.30 There was a spare seat in a booth and when my lunch arrived I quickly took my place lest I have to eat standing up, a habit I would rather avoid.

I thought the booth empty, but when a man cried out in pain it was a great surprise. There sitting in the corner was a character with his leg and foot up on the cushions taking up half the booth.

"Excuse me," I said. "May I." He nodded and I sat down to enjoy my meal.

Now I have never been one to hunker down over my food and prefer to enjoy my meal at a leisurely pace, but this stranger made me feel like I needed to eat quickly and go. He watched as I chewed.

"Roast Beef," I said.

He hurrumphed.

"Very tasty."

He looked at me and narrowed his eyes.

"Poison," he said.

"Poison?" I asked. He clicked a small worn bone through his fingers and drummed it on the table.

"I cannot eat the beef." He pointed to his foot resting on the booth cushion. "Gout," he said and threw back the last of his drink. "It's a curse."

"I'm sure it can be very painful." I said as I ate my potatoes.

"A curse I said. I curse is always painful." He thumped his empty glass on the table, a signal to the bar and another drink was brought over by the barmaid.

"A curse you say." I was intrigued. I had a good two hours up my sleeve and so I said,

"Tell me more."

And this is how he started.

It was love. Love of a woman. I, Captain Erik Van Bootman was in love. He clicked the small bone around his knuckles as he talked.

It was one of those moonlit nights that you only see above the Tropic of Capricorn. A silver that shines over the water and makes a man think of his dreams beyond the horizon. A light that makes you believe that everything is possible and nothing out of reach.

I studied the Captain. His few words surprised me in their poetry. I nodded and tucked into my gravy and peas.

I was a young lad in those days. Full of bravado and adventure and I found it on the sea. I did my time on the ocean going back and forth from the Spice Islands to the Continent. Pepper mainly, bushels of pepper.

He looked at my lunch and pronounced the word again

"Pepper." It has a smell, the green peppercorns. They smell exotic. They smell of half naked women and warm sand. It is a heady perfume for a lad. A heady perfume indeed. He closed his eyes and I could well imagine him remembering the smell.

We also shipped cloves.

Captain Van Bootman shuddered at the thought of cloves. I have to admit I was not a fan of the condiment as it brought back home remedies for toothaches and other ailments that my Mother swore were cured by cloves.

Cloves are the work of the devil. The Captain thumped the table with his fist and the small bone skittled across to my placemat. I looked at the worn object and he reached over and snatched it back and began to wind it once more through his fingers.

But pepper, that is another story. I fell in love with pepper.

I finished my lunch and ordered another drink wanting to hear more.

"In love you say?" I asked.

Aye, in love. Pepper grows from a vine and it winds its self around the tree and the heart.

She was a beauty my pepper. Her father called her Pepper after the plantation that gave him the wealth. And he was a wealthy man, no doubt about that. She was his only and for that blessing he bestowed all his love and devotion to her and her alone.

Pepper was long limbed, brown with dark tresses that were as black as boot polish and as shiny as obsidian. Her eyes glistened with mischief and her smile could make a bird sing.

Her father was rightly proud, but you can imagine how he protected such a beauty.

We all loved Pepper and I'm sure the business did so well because of her. Who wouldn't want a glimpse of Pepper for a hundred bushels? Who could resist a passing smile or a look from the corner of her eye for a bartered price? His pepper crop was no better or worse than all the rest, yet his was the first to be sold, the first to be shipped and the first to be paid off for a glance from Pepper.

She was only 14 or so when I first saw her and I fell in love. I was a lad of 16 you see and love strikes a young heart like a harpoon and doesn't let go, ever.

The Captain stared into the distance and I fancied he was reliving the tale as he talked.

Every moment I could I would jump my berth and head for the hills to see her. She made my young heart race, and I imagined a world with just the two of us in it, nothing else mattered to us and we lived on love.

The Capt'n smiled at me and his craggy face almost looked youthful again.

"A first love?"

Aye, a first love.

At first I kept to the trees and watched her from a distance. She'd comb her hair with a big ol' ivory comb and hum a tune. It was as if she was doing it just for me as I watched. I was too inexperienced in the ways of girls to actually talk to her and the crew badgered me for it, but I didn't care. Pepper was in my heart and there she stayed.

That first year sailing was torture for me. All I could think about was getting back to the islands. Getting back to my Pepper, for in my mind she was already my wife and belonged to me. I picked up a tortoise shell comb for her in the Solomon Islands and planned to give it to her. I rehearsed what I was going to say, how she would react, what that first kiss would taste like. It was all I could think about as we sailed closer and closer to that green pepper cargo. My sailing mates gave me all sorts of advice about women. They filled my head with notions of love and lust and fired my longing for Pepper.

It was raining the day we docked, but nothing could dampen my ardour. As soon as I had finished my seaman duties I ran. I ran until my heart was thumping on the outside of my chest and my legs felt like jelly, but I had to see her and nothing mattered. I had had a year to think about her. A year to dream about her. A year to yearn for her.

When I saw her I could have almost wept. She had turned from a child to a woman in one year. At 15 she was shapely, and had a wicked look about her. It would be a stronger man that I to resist that look. Pepper had found her beauty was a weapon, a barter chip that she could use to break men's hearts, give them hope or destroy their dreams.

I was still a young lad with dreams. I could work hard, carry bushels all day and never feel an ache or pain, helm 24 hours in tropical storms and sleep the sleep of the innocent, but I was no match for Pepper.

She said I could come and visit. Her father would allow it. She took my offering. She gave me hope. A hope that my young heart took for love and I wished that night would never end. We sat on the verandah of her house and drank coconut milk. As the sun began to set she asked me to comb her hair and I knew then I had truly gone to heaven. Her hair was smooth as Chinese silk and smelt of peppercorns and teak, green tea leaves and cinnamon. My craggy seaman's hands were too course for such fineness, but she didn't care. She laughed at my clumsy attempts and said I should continue. She said she had seen me watching her from the garden in another lifetime. She said she had been waiting for me and had dreamed my dreams while I was away.

I was only 17 and I believed her.

"Ah, youth," I said and drank my beer. Van Bootman visibly relaxed as he remembered a time gone by.

Youth, he reiterated.

I visited every evening while we waited for the stevedores to set the cargo. She would let me sit with her. It was enough for my heart as my innocence was my moral compass. We didn't talk of plans or discuss our love but just sat in the cool retreat from the day and basked in each other's love.

Van Bootman stopped his fingers from playing with the bone and looked at me,

That is what I imagined anyway.

The pepper was loaded and consigned and we had to leave. I wanted to stay, but a young man must have the means if he wants to marry, so I steeled myself for one more year of toil. One more year of yearning, before I could offer Pepper a reasonable life.

The night before we cast off I went to her house on the hill and waited. It was empty. I tramped around the grounds and waited some more. She didn't return. It could only have been an emergency that kept us apart on our last night together I thought, and I left her a note written on a small plank of wood. I cut my name deep into the wood and sealed it with a heart. There could be no mistaking my devotion, my love for Pepper.

We cast off and I vowed to save my every penny for a whole year for our union. When the men went out on the town I stayed in my bunk. When we found ourselves in port because of a cyclone brewing I did not go and seek the company of other women. When I turned 18 I shouted the rum and then did extra duties on other boats to make up the kitty. I was steadfast. My diligence was noted by the Captain and I was promoted. It meant more pay and more responsibilities.

And all the while I thought of Pepper. I didn't know if she could read, but I sent her books anyway and letters. I wasn't schooled very much, but my love found the words to write. I sent small gifts from the islands, ribbons for her hair from the city, and silk handkerchiefs from some Chinese fishermen.

We weren't scheduled to go back to the pepper islands for another four months, when I had a bit of luck of sorts. A clipper was without a first mate and headed that way and so I was recommended by my Captain. He knew I was longing for the Islands and first mate was a step up the ladder for me. The clipper, Sorenson J, was a fine boat, and fast. The crew were fair to a newcomer and I began to get excited as the Sorenson J cut through the water getting ever closer to my Pepper. I had a large purse of money in the bank in Sydney and my prospects were excellent. My new Captain had even given me one week shore leave to get my affairs in order.

And was she waiting? I asked.

It was one of those big blows the day we tried to come into the bay. Not quite a cyclone but enough to keep us out in the bay for two days. They were the longest days of my life up until then. I could see the land; smell the earth and the trees. See the birds heading inland and I was on the boat. One of the crew, an old codger called Bowie, who had been around the world and seen everything there is to see took me aside on the first evening and said,
What are you going to do if she says no?

Well, I had never thought of that. It just didn't occur to me that Pepper wouldn't be waiting for me. I loved her and she must love me.
Still the question ran around in my head as I lay on my bunk. But I was in love and so I dismissed my doubts.

Van Bootman took a long draught of beer and stared off into the distance. I ordered another drink and waited.

We finally hauled into port and I scanned the dock for my love. She wasn't there, so I put her absence down to our delay. Once my duties were fulfilled I made my way up the hill. You'd think I would be running as before, but whether it was a premonition, or Bowie's words I cannot say, but I walked. My knapsack was full of trinkets, love tokens and the hope of my future happiness. To get to the Avelez estate there is a winding road that sometimes gives glimpses of the house. Each tantalizing view made my heart skip a beat, so by the time I reached the gardens and the front steps I was, I felt, the luckiest man alive, and the happiest.

The housekeeper answered my knock and then called for Pepper. She strolled out onto the verandah like she had just seen me yesterday, eating a zalacca and looked at me with those dark eyes. The fruit is often called the snake skin fruit with its scale like skin and I felt Pepper had digested some of the qualities of the reptile. I had gone over this meeting so many times in my mind that the reality came as a bit of a shock. I was ready to cut my heart out for her and she was indifferent.

Van Bootman's fingers stopped twiddling the bone and he winced in pain.

She sat down and I laid out my gifts for her. They now felt cheap and gaudy as she cast her eye over them. I watched her distain and Bowie's words came back to haunt me. Pepper seemed bored with the whole charade and so I tried to tempt her to love me. I showed her my bank account.

The Captain once again took up the bone and threaded it though his fingers.

I promised her all of it if only she would make a solemn promise to me. Weren't we in love last season? Didn't we have something that would last a lifetime? Pepper's eyes sparkled with desire. She did love me after all, her reticence only a native shyness. We spent every afternoon together and wished it could be a whole day, but as I still had my duty to Sorensen J. Those afternoons were my dreams realised. We would walk, kiss, hold hands, swim, all the things young lovers do, then one afternoon I bounded up the road and she had changed.

She said she didn't want to see me anymore. I couldn't understand it. For me, nothing had changed. I had decided to ask her to marry me before the Sorensen J departed once again and felt that would seal our fates together, forever. This change in the weather made me bring my plans forward and so I proposed, adding we just needed to ask her father and then we would be engaged. I felt I would do anything to have her.

And her answer? I asked.

Pepper said yes.

And her father?
He was away. She sent word and he accepted me, she said. And to seal the union a promise....as a measure of my good standing...money.

Ah money, I said.

Of course it was nothing to me as long as Pepper loved me. I gave her a promissory note to be cashed at the stevedore. There was to be a party of sorts amongst my ship mates and her family, but the weather intervened and Sorensen J had to leave early as a cyclone was brewing.
We had sealed our fates. She was mine. I would work for one more year then I promised to work on the farm, to raise a family and be happy for the rest of my days.

Van Bootman looked at me and smirked.
I know what you are thinking. She took my money and spurned my love.
I nodded and smiled.
Ah, you do not trust her motives.
No, I said.

I left Sumatra a happy man. I came back a year later to misery.

We docked on a sunny day and I left the crew in charge as I walked up the hill. I had checked my bank statements and the money was still there. She hadn't spent a penny. The house was deserted when I arrived and so I waited. It was late in the afternoon when the housekeeper came back and she was surprised to see me. More than surprised, she was frightened. I asked her what was the problem, but she ran away. So, as there was nothing to do, I trudged back to the boat.

It didn't take the crew long to hear the news and the Captain took me aside to pass on the gossip.

Pepper was married.

Van Bootman thumped his hand down on the table and his gout gave him a stab of pain.

Married, I reiterated.

I could have cried, but I was mad. She had married a clove farmer. My love, my promises, my loyalty meant nothing to her. In my more lucid moments I thanked the heavens that my money was still intact. I cursed her, I wept for her and I reasoned it was an arranged marriage and she had to follow her elders, except her father had given his consent to me. I resolved to go and see the man.

Avelez was a gentle old man. But when I introduced myself it was as if he had heard the name Bootman for the first time. There was no recognition, no joyous consent, no permission. Pepper had fabricated it all.

So did you find her?

I did.

And?

And I wanted to tell her how I hated her. How I loathed her deceit. How I would never love her, but when I saw her I could not. She was more beautiful than ever I remembered her. I felt sorry for her, harnessed to a clove farmer. I said we could run away. We could escape and to that end I gave her all my money. She laughed at my clumsy attempts. She took my money and laughed at me. It was as if she wanted me to make me beg. Although I loved her, her mocking struck my pride and I shouted at her that she was a whore. I told her I had seen her father and the reception I received. We all say things in anger and I demanded an explanation.

How could she have broken her promise, if ever there was one in her mind? I struck her. Just the once, but my action cut deep into my heart. I regretted my actions. I begged her forgiveness. Oh how I begged her to forgive me. I couldn't bear to see her married to cloves. It just wasn't right.

And you know what she did.

I shook my head.

After all I sacrificed for her. After I promised myself to her.

What?

She turned and spat a curse on me. Me, who had loved her for three years. A curse that would follow me around the world and back again.

Van Bootman looked at his foot.

I left that island paradise a broken youth. How could I ever love again?

And the curse? I asked intrigued.

Ah, the curse. A cruel damnation if ever there was one. Every time I would love, it would be snatched from me. I became a Captain and fell in love with Sorensen J. She was my home and a more beautiful boat you never saw on the wind. A reef took her from under me.
I left the sea for the land and found a small island I could call home. I made a life there and was happy. A tsunami took it all away. So I went to sea, but every boat was jinxed. I could not find happiness. No-one would take me on and I drifted the islands and the oceans never settled, never happy. I met a girl, she wasn't demanding and I thought I might have a chance at love. She fell ill, a malaise that left her bedridden, then she died. The family said it was my fault and I suppose it was. Everything I touched was wrenched from me. It was a curse with no cure.

And the bone? I asked looking at his hand.

A talisman from the Aboriginies. They say it keeps the bad away. The bad will work its way out through the toe.

I looked at his foot on the cushion and he winced at my glance.

Did you ever see Pepper again? I was curious to know.

Van Bootman shook his head.

No. A fisherman I knew said she had left her husband, taken a lover, then another. There was a string of unhappy men like the rope of pearls that she wore around her neck.

When will you be free? I nodded towards his foot.

Erik Van Bootman shrugged his shoulders. Perhaps when I love my pain as much as I loved Pepper, then it will be wrenched from me.

It was a logic that fitted the tale.

Plate V

Boy

The winds that blow in North Queensland are sometimes called the Mango winds, and the heat that precedes the winds and the impending wet can set a man's mind to madness.

I was waiting for the last transport to head south before the monsoons came. It was while I waited in the Magee Hotel in Collinsville, Faraday the hotel publican, told me the story of Boy.
Faraday settled back, and with a fresh rum and a cigarette, began.

Murray Webb, some said, was born in the saddle. His life, if you cared to inquire, consisted of horses and cattle and not much else. Spider, as he was known in the dusty parts of the Australian north where no man goes by choice, was a stockman. A ringer with a reputation. Rumours followed him around like the relentless flies. Men who knew Spider knew enough to keep their distance. He may have been the best drover this side of the border. He might have killed every wild dog or dingo within a 50 mile radius of the station, but all that anyone could really say with any certainty was that Spider didn't have a merciful bone in his body.

What had happened to Murray in his youth had coloured his life, and the scars of suffering ran so deep they touched his heart and left their mark.

Spider came to Collinsville looking for work. The drought had been hard, and the wind had laid bare the backbone of the land. Men wandered from one town to the next in search of a wage to stem their hunger and keep their self esteem. Honest labour can make a man and the lack of it can break him. Spider was on the hunt for a job. The one station that still had a few head of cattle and some feed needed a drover.

Sizzling Rock Station stood out in the shire as an example of good land and better management. The Stenton family had steadily built the land around the cattle and because they held the water, not much happened that didn't have their stamp on it. The last leading hand died, some said of bad blood. No-one wanted to say more, but plenty had an idea where the bad blood came from and none wanted to say. Tanner had run the cattle for Sizzlin' Rock for about ten years and he knew just about every inch of that property. Ol' man Stenton used to say he was a chip off the ol' block and we all knew what he meant. Tanner had the ol' man in him alright, but, well, he wasn't strong enough and when the bush calls 'em, the black in 'em can't resist. Tanner went bush for a bit and when he finally came back well... the mixed blood always has a way of testing a man's mind and strengths and Tanner wasn't up to the fight. The white in him fought the black and he just up and died. Laid down on his bed, closed his eyes and never woke up.

There was pragmatism in Faraday's words. Here was a man who had run an outback pub and probably seen more than his fair share of life at the sharp end, and yet he spoke the words with no more consideration than reading a label on a bottle.

"He just never woke up," Faraday reiterated and supped his rum.

Lance Stenton the businessman, was on the lookout for a hand. Lance Stenton, the father, kept his feelings to himself. But we all knew it would have to be someone with talent to take the place of Tanner at Sizzlin' Rock. So when Spider came into town Stenton sought him out. Some fellas, no matter what their ugly past, just seem to land on their feet. Spider was like that. He stood over six foot, and in the saddle he towered over most men. He had a crag of a face, like a weathered rock. His dark eyes squinted at everything and he carried a permanent sneer the way some men carry a cigarette on their lip.

Faraday looked at me earnestly, "I never saw him take off his hat, not ever. I don't think he'd look the same without that hat. It was just part of him, part of what he was, and what he had become."

I took a long draught of my cold beer and watched the ceiling fan endlessly turn, giving little comfort, except to the flies that followed it. Faraday continued.

Whatever drove Spider it was relentless. He'd no more feelings for his fellow man than the stray dogs he would shoot, and the only saving grace he possessed was his way with cattle. He just knew how to handle 'em. What they'd be thinkin' and what they wanted. It was, some said, a gift. So it was that Lance Stenton engaged Murray Webb for a muster, and possible further employment at Sizzlin' Rock Station.

Lance's second man was Boy. Boy had grown up at Sizzlin' Rock and when Tanner up and died Boy expected to get the job. No-one knew where Boy had come from; just walked right out of the bush and Tanner took him in. There was something about Boy, a kinda feeling that he could see right through you, that made you look away. It was as if he was too old for the skin he was in, and so he kinda became invisible to the folks around these parts, lest he look too deep into a man's heart. Whenever Tanner came to town, Boy wasn't far behind, but he never drank. Tanner would take a lemonade out to him, but Boy, even when he was well above the age, never set foot in the bar. It's like that sometimes. The black fellas are afraid if they start they'll never stop. Tanner preferred to drink outside with Boy rather than up at the bar. I guess the colour of your skin is a dictate of your friends, no matter what's on the inside.

As a magistrate I knew the truth in these words, having witnessed prejudice many times on both sides of the fence.

Sizzlin' Rock is a large station. The cattle are feral most of the year so it's a long haul when they bring them in. Tanner used to go bush living on what he could find and it was a natural thing for him and Boy. I heard he killed a roo with his bare hands once, but what is the truth and what is drink talkin', sometimes it's hard to tell.
There were a couple of other blacks in the saddle the day Spider left for the muster and you could have cut the air with a knife as they rode through town. If Boy had a fight in him he kept it close to his chest. If Spider had any hope of those blokes following him he needed to make a stand.

Faraday drew heavily on his cigarette then flicked the stub out the window in a practiced movement. I wondered how many butts lay on the other side from a lifetime behind the bar.

So the new man chose his moment, and just as he passed the Hotel, he pulled his whip from his saddle and cracked it over Boy. That leather just caught the shirt and no more, but it was enough. Boy never said a word, but they all knew who was boss that day.

But that wasn't the first time they had met. When Spider first blew into town he walked right past Boy on the verandah, but he hadn't downed his first drink when he came over all queer.

"Somebody walk over your grave?" I asked.

"Nah, just the heat," he said, "and the damn wind."

"Yeah – the wind," I said to him. It can make sane men crazy. I've seen it before, but I could tell it was something more than just the wind, and all the while Boy just sat there, not sayin' a word."

It's a hard life on the land, but for those fellas that choose it, it's second nature. The team found their head of beef and started to bring them home, but there was trouble brewing. Spider began to goad Boy.

Some men would snap. I've seen it at the bar. A word said that goes over the line and the first punch is thrown. Some men like a fight it clears the air, and you can get on with living. But Boy wouldn't fight. He wouldn't take the bait. No matter what insult, what remark, Spider came away with nothing. Spider went from the antagonist to the victim. With every snub he felt slighted. It was a twisted logic that left him wanting revenge. It all came to a head at Sizzling Rock.

It's a flat piece of rock stuck out in the middle of bloody nowhere. A black kind of rock that just shouldn't be there. A strange sort of place that can make you scratch the back of your neck, like something's just not right. It catches the sun by day and by God you could fry an egg on it.

Faraday leaned in close and confided,

I went there once. As a lad, just before the wet. It was one of those days when it's too hot even to breathe. Your shirt sticks to your back and you wonder if you are already dead and this is your private hell. I can tell you, it's a crazy business waiting for the rains. So I get to the rock and it's still. Not a breath of wind. Just the sun. The rock was so hot it was all shimmery and it made you wonder if it was really there or just one of those mirages. The doorway to Hades. The blacks keep away from it, and I don't blame them. I wanted to touch it and was just plucking up the courage when it started to rain. Just a few drops at first and as they hit the rock it was like they didn't want to be there. The water was steaming, and dancing to get off that rock. Sizzlin' and steaming. That rock just spat the water back and then it gave a moan. A low rumbling moan. I tell you I ran so fast I beat the rain back to town.

Faraday lit a smoke and sat back.

"Like something's just not right, stuck out in the middle of nowhere," he finished, and dragged on his cigarette.

When Spider's droving party finally got back to town it only took two schooners at the bar for the news to hit.

Boy was missing.

The talk was, Boy had gone walkabout. Lance Stenton said it was bound to happen one day and left it at that, content with his profit. The other two men in the muster left town pretty quick and the story of what really happened went with them, or so we thought.

The wind found its way inside the pub and worried the naked light bulbs hanging over the bar.

Faraday looked up and their weak light flicked over his features as they swung. The air was oppressive, yet expectant with rain. The few customers in the bar, sat silent and still, with nothing to do but sweat.

"I wish it would bloody rain."It was a sentiment we all agreed upon. Faraday wiped his brow with his shirt sleeve and poured a beer.

With the wet just around the corner, the cattle in, and not much else to do, Spider took to drinking. He hadn't been in the top end before and it's not an easy thing. It can make a man crazy for some relief. The heat can sap your energy until you've nothing left but a bad temper or a mighty thirst. Spider had both. He drank, and when he drank he talked. We all listened.

He's the kinda man that has been all over and done things some of us could only imagine. He told us about mustering in the Kimberlys and having to fight off crocs that wanted the cattle. He'd tell us about hunting roos so big they could rip a horse to pieces and then on other days he describe the outback so vividly we all could feel the dust and the heat and the empty spaces that make your eyes hurt and your heart ache for the horizon. He took us to the gorges in the centre where pools of water lay still and deep, where the shadows are cool and the chasms echo your words and dreams. We rode with him to the Blue Mountains and the snow and listened as he described the bitter wind, the cold ground and the ache in your bones that long for the sun. But most days he talked about killing dogs, until, about a week into his binge, he let it slip he had killed a man.

No one wanted to believe him. After all he had been on a bender for a good week. But people round here were quick to put two and two together and come up with Boy.

Word got around to Sizzling Rock Station and Ol' man Stenton came to town to figure it out. It was a stinking hot day when Lance walked into the bar, took off his hat and wiped his brow with his shirt sleeve and called for Spider. Spider had been renting a room upstairs and he slowly made his way down and put his money on the bar. Lance just stood there and watched that craggy face. Spider never blinked.

"Where the bloody hell is Boy?" Lance said. Sweat was dripping down his face and he looked just about ready to melt.

"Dunno."

"Bullshit."

"He just fuckin' walked off the job." Spider said and took a swig of his beer.

"That's not what I heard Mr. Webb."

"Well you heard wrong Mr. Stenton."

Ol' Stenton was just about to have a go at Spider, when I had to reach for the baton.

"There'll be no fightin' in my bar gentlemen. Take it outside." Lance stormed off and Spider called for a refill, but we all had a creepy sort of feelin' then that something wasn't right, Spider wasn't even sweating.

The rains eventually came and Spider moved on. Ol' man Stenton wouldn't have him on the block.

He said he'd have him arrested if he came around these parts again, but as there was no body or anyone to talk, it all just became a good yarn on those days when there is nothing much to do except wait for the rains.

I wondered if that was the end of the story when Faraday gave me a long stare and asked,
"Do you believe in ghosts Mr Weatherness?" I supped my drink and remained a fence sitter.
Faraday lit another cigarette and began again.

It was a full year, and a lot can happen in a year up here, but one year to the day Boy disappeared he walked into town and sat down on the front verandah. Someone suggested we call Stenton, but I wasn't so sure. I felt that prickle on the back of my neck and it didn't seem right, so I said just leave it alone. If he wanted to go to the station well that would be his business. It was a mighty hot day that day and we watched as Boy sat not drinking his lemonade the missus had taken out to him. He sat there all day with his back to the wall until the sun dipped behind Wallunup ridge, then he just got up and left. It was then we saw the scars on his back. Now I've seen plenty of roughed up men in my time, but these scars were vicious. Three strikes across his back.

Faraday held up three fingers to emphasize the point.
The sun casts long shadows and can blind a man if he's trying to look too hard into the future...or past. Boy just walked towards the sunset and try as I might to

follow him with a squint, he was gone. For thee days he came to the pub. One the third day we had quite a crowd in and Ol' man Stenton came to town. No-one could get Boy to talk and he just sat. It was creepy and there were plenty of stories going round about his visit, but none that came near to the truth. Nothing stays secret for long up here and Spider soon heard the stories. Someone had seen him in Alice Springs and news came back that he was drinking hard.

Faraday flicked another dead butt out the window and looked at the flyblown calendar on the wall.
"It was a year of terrific rains. The ground just drank it up and the cattle grew fat. People said they had never seen it so good. Not for a long time, and Ol' man Stenton was rubbing his hands together. We were all feeling pretty good and then Boy arrived.
The barman looked at me and expected some sort of reaction. I duly obliged with a question.
"And was he the same." Faraday nodded.
"Exactly the same. He came the next year and by then we were kinda expecting it.
"And Spider?" I asked.
"He picked up a bit of work here and there, but something changed him. He was withering away."
Spider had heard of Boy and it was a festering sore. It ate into his bones and sapped his strength leaving him a shambling wreck even though he was only in his 50's. The word was he worried himself to death.

"He died three years to the day." Faraday swung his head over to the calendar. "Three years to the day Boy disappeared. And then," Faraday absently picked his teeth with a toothpick, "And then Boy stopped coming. Just like that."

The clock above the bar chimed the hour and I jumped then felt a strange tingling sensation on the back of my neck. I rubbed it and wiped my brow.

"Hot eh?"

"Yes."

"I wish it would bloody rain. Waiting for the rains can make a man crazy." Faraday said then lit another cigarette.

Plate VI

Martin Swinburne

Martin Swinburne liked the sound of his own voice. He was a short man with bland features and a thinning head of blonde hair that he judiciously combed over a growing bald patch. His mouth contained less than was God given teeth, which were yellowing and congregated at the front.

I have often been told I have a face that people take for trustworthy. As the possessor of such a face, people tell me things. Secrets, life histories, lies and more. Martin, in the matter of one beer told me his life story.

From the moment Martin found he was always on the outer of the 'in' crowd he had been trying to get 'in'. So, in his efforts, he espoused on any and every subject without so much as a small modicum of knowledge. But, for all his 'attributes' the one that most remembered Mr. Swinburne to his neighbours, acquaintances and family was that after 40 years of marriage he could still make his wife cry.

Violet Swinburne, it could be said, was a stoic character with a gentle disposition. Violet had been branded plain as a child and in her later years the description wound itself so completely around her there could be no other. She had a small round face framed by lank hair. A permanent wave might have been added, but it didn't lift the overall effect. Her chin just managed to make an appearance and then quickly disappeared to be taken over by a scrawny neck. It was Mr. Swinburne's habit to remind his wife of the fact that she was plain, and he could have had any number of belles in his youth. No-one bothered to ask the obvious question as to why he chose Violet, as the underlying feeling was, Martin's 'any number' began and ended with one; Violet.

The Swinburnes had not produced offspring, a fact that was oft repeated by Martin, who, with no more knowledge of doctoring than the corner shopkeeper, laid the blame squarely on Violet's shoulders, or hips, if his conversation was to be believed.

I met the Swinburnes by accident one Saturday, as an interloper, hanging on the merest invitation to attend their wedding anniversary. The occasion was their 40th and I supposed it to be a jolly affair. Mr. Swinburne sidled up to me in the bar and slapped me on the back.

"Have another," he indicated my whisky. I could see he had made a head start on the beer and now he swayed as he hung onto the rail worn shiny by many hands over the years.

"Martin Swinburne, I'm with the bank," he held out a grubby paw with eaten fingernails and sporting a large opal ring. I nodded and introduced myself and the die was cast.

The ring, he explained, was owned by a celebrity who relinquished it when his funds or popularity ran dry. The name was thrown around in the hope of exciting interest, but didn't hit the mark. Swinburne elaborated on the connection, but you can only drop a name so many times before it refuses to get up again. The bartender smiled in my direction, and I imagined him wishing me luck.

Martin gulped his brew and with his dirty hand and a loose invitation pulled me to the function room. I glanced back at the bartender in the hope of rescue, but he just shrugged his shoulders and continued to wipe the bar with a well used rag.

The back room at the Julia Creek Hotel was decorated with every expense spared. A few forlorn balloons adorned the obligatory picture of the sheep shearer; a table was laid with white linen and contained a cake, a very small cake, and some mismatched plates. One cheap almost pathetically singular bottle of bubbly stood unopened next to the cake with about a dozen glassed for company. With some source of pride Martin directed me to look at the cake.

"40 year," he said, "40 bloody years." It was then I noticed the woman sitting in the corner. She seemed to blend into the room's furniture.

"Vi," Swinburne pointed with his stubby finger at the figure. His gesture was one of indifference and had no more thought than someone pointing out a familiar object, like a bookcase or an electric fan. She nodded and with head down mumbled,

"Violet," her hands wringing the life from a hanky in her lap. I smiled and bowed and then Swinburne directed my attention once again to the cake.

"Cost a fortune," he said standing over the decorated cake which to my untrained eye looked homemade. The number 40 was played out with candles and they perched on the top amid tinned peaches and cream. The weather can be unkind in the tropics, and the cream was beginning to sag, precipitating a slide of the topping to one side. Violet stood up and walked over to the table as we admired the treat. She smiled and lowered her eyes and I knew my suspicions were correct.

"I made it," she said. I said something appropriate and congratulated her on the anniversary. Standing there in the empty room I felt a pang of sorrow for the woman. I knew no more of her than her name and her cake making abilities, but I felt she deserved more. As a magistrate I'd seen all of life's ills, but Mrs Swinburne touched by sensibilities. Her attempt at making an occasion included putting on her makeup and jewellery. The makeup could not disguise her plain looks, and her jewels were a dime a dozen, as the Americans so aptly describe. Mr Swinburne interrupted our introduction by pointing out the cost of the room, the cost of the drink and the sheer extravagance, not forgetting to mention that as a

Captain of Industry he was well able to effort such thing, but it was an extravagance all the same.

I finished my whisky and made the pretence of having to go to the bar, when Martin, with a flick of his hand directed Violet to fetch my refill.

"No, that's not necessary," I protested, but Violet was already obeying the order and began to walk out the door.

"And tell them to put it on my tab," Martin yelled after the receding figure. I was then informed of his standing in the hotel and his extensive credit, which was just for him alone.

"Working in the bank has some advantages," he said. The tale would have been believable except for the quick glance I gave to the glass doors and saw Violet handing over some money and waiting for the change. It seemed Mr Swinburne's credit didn't extend to a second round. Violet just caught my glance through the door and I thought I detected a smirk. It might have been the light, but I felt that she was enjoying the moment when Martin and his exaggerations were found to be false.

"We're just waiting for the guests," Mr Swinburne said by way of explanation at the empty room. "Everyone is fashionably late these days." I nodded and took my drink from Mrs Swinburne.

"Thank you," I said.

"No trouble at all," she said, then walked back to her seat in the corner and sat down, her job complete. I wondered in this small town how many guests might arrive. Julia Creek wasn't what you would describe as a thriving metropolis. It still had dirt roads and besides the bank was about as devoid of society as a place could get.

"So what do you do?" Mr. Swinburne asked me. I have always tried to steer away from a direct reply to this rather irksome question. To say I'm a Magistrate conjures up all sorts of demons for the public. They feel they are being grilled or shy away with guilty looks, so I said I was in human management. It wasn't altogether a lie. Martin then proceeded to tell me all about human management and how he had held several rather high profile jobs in the position. I glanced over to Mrs Swinburne who held her hanky up to her mouth and I rather fancy I saw her titter.

"Martin, wasn't that the job where they said they had never met anyone like you before...ever." Violet said. Martin shot a withering stare over to his wife and said something about not reaching his potential. We stood about for a minute and then someone came in the door just in time to break the awkward moment.

"Oh sorry, I thought this was the Blinkly party." Mr Swinburne's shoulders slumped as the potential guest made a hasty retreat.

"No one is ever on time these days." he said and he looked at the glass door closing and then at his watch, "Never mind. I expect they will all come at once. We have a lot of friends in the town." He seemed to try to be convincing himself rather than me. Then he went on to describe how his friends were of the upper echelon of society, and included the bank manager, another who owned the newspaper and how many lawyers he knew. I nodded out of politeness and looked to the glass door. It remained stubbornly closed for the next fifteen minutes as I listened to Martin's discourse on how time poor everyone is these days and people with high profile lives have a very hard time just trying to get time to relax.

"Shall I put the bubbly back in the fridge?" Violet asked as the clock ticked on. Martin rounded on his wife,

"It's champagne not bubbly. I don't know why you insist on calling it bubbly." She shrank back from the attack and her eyes glassed over with tears. He took a deep breath,

"It's not as if I haven't explained it often enough. Some people are just thick and I'm bound to say you seem to be one of them Violet. You just don't listen." Then he turned to me and said,

"I asked for Champagne as it is a special occasion. The barman could see I knew a thing or two about the quality of his cellar and no one can pull the wool over my eyes. I could have been a wine taster. I was told my palate is exceptional for the nuances of wine. But well...we all make choices in life." He looked over to his wife and glared. Violet wiped her glassy eyes and studied the floor.

"But I thought Champagne was only from France. That bottle was from the Barossa Valley." Violet almost whispered the words, but the effect was to make Martin roll his eyes skyward as if to say all women are idiots and we just have to put up with it. I felt the effect was to belittle Martin and she had scored.

Martin and I looked at the clock and then the doors. As the awkward moment grew into several minutes I coughed and was about to bid my farewell when Violet stood up, tucked her hanky in the sleeve of her cardigan, took the bottle off the table and walked out of the room. I longed to follow her and escape, but Martin grabbed my arm and began,

"You know she used to be a pianist. Grand piano and all that. But when she married me she gave it all away. They said she could have been a great soloist." He waited for my response but I couldn't think of anything to say.

"I know, why don't we get her to play when she comes back." Martin seemed genuinely proud of his wife's ability. I looked at the bar through the glass door and saw Violet knocking back a drink and talking to the barman. She had managed to extricate herself and it didn't look like she was coming back anytime soon. I cursed my upbringing and my good manners which hindered my escape.

"She can play anything you like. I'll tell her she must play. We men must put our foot down sometimes, eh?" I wondered at his capacity to brawl out his wife and then command her to do a party turn in the same breath. He looked at the upright piano standing in the corner of the function room. It was being used as a storage table for the cutlery and table linen and looked like it hadn't been played in a long time.

"Oh, that's alright." I said, "She probably doesn't want to play at her own celebration. Much like a busman's holiday." I secretly wondered if Violet's prowess on the piano was just another of Martin grandiloquent remarks.

"She'll play. I'll make sure of that." Mr Swinburne pursed his lips and then finished his beer. "Another?" he indicated my empty glass.

"I think I shall retire."

"Nonsense Mr Weatherness the night is young." I tried to protest, but he had a firm grip on my upper arm and was ushering me to the bar. I imagined the scene when he discovered Violet sitting on a bar stool, smoking a cigarette and talking to the local talent and so steeled myself for the confrontation.

"Really, I'd rather just finish up." I said and shrugged off his grip. We walked through the door and I took a deep breath. Martin stood and surveyed his domain. He coughed and hoped someone would look up, but his effort at an entrance to the bar was unnoticed.

"Violet," he shouted and walked over to his wife. I waited for the floor to open up and swallow me whole. Violet looked over to Martin and blew out a pall of smoke. With a few drinks under her belt she had shrugged off the timid housewife and seemed to have gained a backbone.

"Yes?"

"Mr Weatherness wants you to play." I protested. Violet raised one eyebrow. For all her plain looks her face could express any number of emotions. Now I felt she had the upper hand and was enjoying toying with her husband.

"Does he?"

"And I said you would. So it's settled then." Martin hunted around the bar for a piano. He saw a decrepit one in the corner of the room and made a bee line for the instrument.

Violet looked to me and I began to sweat under her scrutiny

"And you're wondering Mr Weatherness if I can really play or is Martin just...". I started to wonder why I felt sorry for the woman when she obviously enjoyed baiting her husband. And after 40 years she was the expert. Her sardonic smile made me wince. She gulped a double shot and pursed her lips.

"Vi," Martin shouted over the heads of the locals. "She's a concert pianist you know." he added trying to instil some excitement to the disinterested drinkers. One or two looked up then went back to their beers. I was trapped, yet intrigued by the relationship of the the Swinburnes. Martin was a bore of the biggest order, yet he was harmless, but Violet was the dark horse. She had practiced her art of put downs and slights, I would suggest, over many years. I began to feel sorry for the poor smuck. Martin and Violet deserved one another.

He beckoned his wife over to the piano and she dutifully slid off the stool and sauntered over to the instrument.

"What's it to be Mr Weatherness?" she asked over the crowd. Suddenly all eyes were on me and and I froze. I opened my mouth but nothing would come out.

"Mr. Weatherness?" Martin repeated. "Vi is top notch. Anything at all."

"What's it to be?" Violet asked again. I looked around for some help. The barman averted his gaze and the bar suddenly hushed.

"Scott Joplin, Maple leaf Rag." I blurted out. Martin stood on a chair and held his beer aloft.

"Scott Joplin it is. Vi?" He looked at his wife and I fancied I saw a spark of pride. If Martin didn't have any kudos himself he wasn't shy of getting it off his wife's back. Violet parked a cigarette in the corner of her mouth and flexed her fingers.

The melody that thumped out of that old Steinway piano was little short of amazing. Violet played with vigour and her virtuosity was boundless. From Rag time to Jazz, to old music hall favourites, she knew them all. Martin was in his element bouncing off the accolades and telling anyone and everyone that they had been together for 40 years.

It was very late when the publican finally kicked out the last of the revellers. As he stood in the doorway Violet stubbed out her last cigarette and threw back the remains of her gin and tonic. Martin swayed next to the piano and said,

"She was a concert pianist once you know." I watched as he looked down at Violet sitting at the piano and it seemed to me he was weighing up her value. Violet looked at her fingers folded in her lap.

"Well that's all for tonight." the landlord said, then looked at me and added, "I guess you see all sorts in your travels, being a Magistrate an' all that." Martin pricked up his ears.

"Magistrate?" I nodded and quickly added,

"Well thank you for a wonderful evening. Congratulations on your anniversary. I'll be off now." I proceeded to the stairs and my welcoming bed and walked past the function room. The cake had given up and lay drunkenly in two halves on the linen tablecloth, the balloons sagged and any suggestion of the 40 years being happy ones was dispelled with one look at the dismal scene.

"Good night Your Lordship," Martin called. I could have corrected him. I could have pointed out I was only a magistrate, but as I climbed the stairs I imagined I heard Martin espousing his connection to a Judge and a guest at his wedding anniversary no less. I could easily hear Violet's rejoinder and thought their symbiotic relationship would last another 40 years.

Plate VII

Lionel Arkwright.

As the wet encroaches on the landscape what was once dry and brown becomes verdant green. There is a burgeoning of growth and life seems to spring once again from presumed dead shrubs, trees and grass. The other consequence to the beginning of the wet is the humidity and its close association with mould. When I travel I try to keep my clothes dry and clean, but mould attacks insidiously and so I found myself at a draper shop in Yungaburra in the Atherton tablelands.

Messers Rockwell & May catered for all the needs of the district. From farm shirts to ladies lace they could put their hands on just about anything at a price. I walked the store marvelling at the extent of the stock. Things to take stones out of shoes, hair tonics, lace doilies, belt buckles depicting cattle, leather strapping and the list went on. I needed a white shirt, but what I received was a tale of obsession.

Mr Rockwell, a man of taste and distinction, by the look of the cut of his suit and his tie, fluttered around me as I looked for a 15 1/2 neck. He was a small man with a dower round face. Not particularly handsome, but he had an attentive stare that made you feel like he was interested in your purchases alone. A bonus, I would have thought, for a shop keeper. He knew of my occupation, nothing gets past a shopkeeper for gossip, and I could see he wanted advice on the cheap. I sighed and inclined my head in acceptance of the inevitable. I often wonder if I was a butcher, would people want a cut of meat laid on the table while in casual conversation. Why it is that people try to wheedle some free legal advice I have yet to figure out. Mr Rockwell hovered and gushed.

A man in your position, he started, would need a few white shirts. Being in high office you need to set an example. I would suppose you know quite a bit about the law Mr Weatherness. Rockwell smiled and I answered,

Yes.

So you would know all the ins and outs of these things? He was fishing for an invitation and I could have baited him for a good twenty minutes, but I put him out of his misery.

Oh, I know enough Mr Rockwell, I said. Did you have a particular nut of a problem? It was all he needed. He shooed away his young assistant, telling him to watch the shop and then he began.

I'll start at the beginning shall I? He said.

Yes do, I answered.

Mr Lionel Arkwright was an uncle on my mother's side. A beefy fellow, he was practical and forthright, giving his no nonsense opinion on anything and everything. There was nothing Lionel Arkwright didn't pontificate on at great length. Such a man was to be avoided if you didn't have a spare hour up your sleeve.

I briefly wondered if Mr Rockwell had inherited the family trait and tried to avoid looking at my pocket watch. Rockwell warmed to his task and continued.

He worked at the local council depot, keeping track of their vehicles and that sort of thing, lived in a modest, plain, highset house in Yungaburra, had never married, had regular habits and was a part of the local town as the pub or the cinema. He had lived in Yungaburra all his life; the Arkwrights have been here since they first started logging. The Rockwells a little bit longer.

I thought I detected a slight case of one-upmanship in the family tree.

Mr Rockwell looked around his shop for customers and when satisfied the place was empty he took a deep breath and launched himself into the story.

It all started on a spring day not long after the annual local agricultural and horticultural show had taken place. We look forward to the sideshows, the thrills and the fairy floss. It isn't a big affair, but the excitement is good enough for our tastes. The Showies park their carts on the local oval near the pub and give the town a taste of adventure for sixpence. Lionel had gone to the show in anticipation of seeing the cattle, watching the show jumping and wood chopping events.

Rockwell puffed up his chest. We have prize winning dairy cattle this way, he said. The pasture is rich for dairy. I began to get a feel for Mr Rockwell and his need for aggrandisement.

Uncle Lionel he had a opinions on everything and he was sure he'd spot a prize heifer, a winner in dressage and would boast he could chop at a decent pace in his youth and be champion if he had had the time. Of course he had attended many shows in the past and nothing untoward had happened, but this time he took umbrage at a sideshow game of chance.

Rockwell frowned. Something to do with the quoits being too small for the block of wood. A ruckus was the result. My Uncle was not used to being told what to do, especially by a blow-in and he had to be held back by some of the wood choppers, lest he do something he might regret. The upshot was Arkwright was ejected from sideshow alley. But, if the town gossip is to be believed, a curse was spat at his broad back for good measure.

I was left to digest this piece of information. After a short interval Rockwell began again.

The sideshows are run by itinerants, showies who live by their own code. They don't fit in and usually keep themselves to themselves. Things go missing when they are around and you have to be careful. Not to be trusted, but they give a small respite from the everyday when the show comes to town.

Mr Rockwell fiddled with the display of hats and threw a look at his assistant, then he went on.

Lionel was not one to dabble in anything less than practical, so he forgot the incident and that was that -you'd think. Well it was, until one night he heard a knocking at his front door and when he opened it he found no-one there. His front steps were empty. No-one in the street, no wind to set the knocker, but on looking down he saw a small cockroach on the welcome mat which was on the landing. Lionel stomped on the insect and put the knock down to the scant wind.

It was a few days later when Lionel was about to go out, he opened the front door and there on the mat was a cockroach. It stood its ground and he swore it looked up at him. Anyone else might have been spooked by the coincidence, but to Lionel it was a small matter to flick it into the garden and he would have done just that, except something made him stop. He looked at the insect and thought he saw a small sign of recognition. This was the same cockroach. The same small insect he had stomped on the other evening. He took his size 11 boot and squashed the insect so completely it was unrecognisable. Then he took the squished remains and threw them in the rubbish and for good measure he emptied the fire place of ash into the bin. And that was the end of that -or so he thought.

Rockwell drew breath in a theatrical manner and I waited.

Now Arkwright was not a suspicious man at all, but something made him question his judgement that day. A feeling that he shouldn't have done it.

Mr Rockwell picked at an imaginary piece of fluff on his sleeve.

A feeling that things could only get worse, he said. And they did.

It was a week to the day that there was a knock at Arkwright's front door.

I raised my eyebrows and Rockwell nodded. There on the door mat was a cockroach. Just standing there. Well you can imagine the thoughts that went through Lionel's mind. It was too much to be a coincidence. Too much to suppose he had to ring the exterminators. Too much to bare.

The roach didn't scare easily. Lionel, the practical man, who in usual circumstances was as ordinary as bread and butter, was too afraid to kill it. He shooed it with no effect. He prodded it, but it did not move. So he did the only thing he felt would protect his sanity. He picked it up - put it in a matchbox and took it inside until he could figure the thing out. Arkwright left the box in the kitchen and promised himself that he would take the roach for a nice long drive in the morning. A good many miles, and that would be the end of that - or not.

The very next day he took that matchbox, not daring to look inside, and drove his car, an Austin, way out of town along the road that leads to Mount Hypipamee. Rockwell stopped.

Have you been to the crater Mr Weatherness?

I conceded I had not.

It is a deep hole. There are several around the district. Lake Eacham is one and Lake Barrine another. At the crater he threw a stone to gauge the depth, then when satisfied it was good and deep he tied the matchbox to a stone and threw it into the volcanic crater. It would be the finish of the strange occurrences once and for all - or so he presumed.

Rockwells fondness for hanging endings reminded me of the radio serials which are so popular.

Mr Rockwell glanced around the shop until he spied his assistant trying to look busy. They exchanged a nod and Rockwell turned to me to continue.

It is a family trait that the Arkwrights have been sound sleepers.

Mr Rockwell once again explained that Lionel Arkwright was his uncle on his mother's side. Family lore has it that as a baby Lionel slept right through a cyclone.

I nodded in approval at the capacity, knowing how hard it is to get a good healthy eight hours of rest.

Well now Arkwright couldn't sleep. He tried. He paced. He drank warm milk. He drank the brandy that should go in the warm milk and still a good night's sleep eluded him. Night after night he could only catch a few hours, then he would be awake. The doctor prescribed pills and Lionel, usually a cynic when it came to illness, Lionel the man who often said half the illness in the world was only in the head of the patient, jumped at the medication like a dying man.

The draper smoothed out a bolt of material with his fine fingers and ran them over the feel of the cloth. I don't take pills myself. We Rockwell's are made of sterner stuff. I could see he was distancing himself from the Arkwright side of the family.

And did the pills fix the problem? I asked.

Well... Lionel followed the instructions on the label, one a night and all was going well, until he started to dream. Now he wished to stay awake for the dreams were more in the nature of nightmares.

Rockwell paused then whispered, nightmares. And what was contained in these nightmares? He asked the rhetorical question.

I shrugged.

Cockroaches - well only one. Rockwell slapped his hand down on his cutting table.

He had a dream that a cockroach owned his house. Not only owned it, but was in residence - sitting in his front room, reading his book, listening to his radio and smoking his pipe. So real was the dream that Lionel Arkwright took steps.

Rockwell stopped and shook his head. He came in close. They say, in the family, that the Arkwright side have always been a little eccentric. It doesn't come over to the Rockwells. We are a strong line.

Steps? I asked.

Steps, he reiterated. Lionel went to the hardware store and purchased brown tape, wax wood and nails.

And what did he do with his purchases? Rockwell asked me. I shrugged my shoulders.

He began to board up his house. You can imagine what went through the mind of the family. Lionel had lost his marbles. He had succumbed to the Arkwright hereditary. There was talk of an uncle once going loopy. A cousin who saw strange birds in his front yard. An aunt who talked to the radio. It was bound to happen, the family said - inevitable some suggested. But Lionel had never shown any of the symptoms. Never had a flicker of a twitch, never talked to an imaginary friend. He was such a stout fellow.

The draper shrugged his shoulders. You never can tell, the family decided.

Meanwhile, Lionel began to lock himself in. More than lock himself in - to seal himself in his house. He fetched a large ladder and the windows and doors were boarded up. Then sealed with paper and wax from the inside. The air vents were waxed shut, even the letterbox was nailed tight such was the paranoia of Lionel Arkwright.

There was a bit of talk in the town about the goings on at Maple Street. As the gossip spread the family had to do something.

We tried to coax him out. Tried to make him see reason, cajole him to open the door, but he was stubborn and refused.

Rockwell looked at me as if in forgiveness. What could the family do but call the authorities. We all went over to his house and they, the local police, tried to get him to come out. We spoke to him through the door, but he wasn't for moving. In the end they said they couldn't force him to open the door. They couldn't arrest him, for there was no crime, and suggested he would come out when he was hungry. It wasn't what we wanted to hear, but what could we do. Every avenue we had tried, failed.

I nodded with the sentiment of the police knowing full well a man's home is his castle.

Lionel refused all of our advances. Rockwell brought me to one side and whispered, we didn't know about the 'thing' then - he made his fingers into bugs legs and skitted them across the cutting table.

Well weeks went by and Lionel festered in his high set house with well kept gardens and its own water supply. He lived on the same street as the school and children began to throw stones at the house. These sorts of things turn into local folk lore pretty quickly. The children had decided that Arkwright was a mad hermit who ate nothing but house geckoes. It was quite distressing for the family. Things began to look grim as Christmas approached and so the family had a meeting. It was decided someone should break in and take charge. There was more than the family name at stake. It was a matter of saving him from himself. Someone had to go.

Rockwell straightened up and stood to attention.

You? I enquired.

Me, he replied.

We gathered tools from a cousin's shop and one Sunday set upon the front door. I wasn't keen on the break and enter because the house is a solid one and you don't get workmanship like that these days. But break the door down we did. There was no protest as the wood shattered. No yell or scream as we wrenched the nails from the frame and made an opening.

And? I asked.

And I crawled inside. Everything was neat and tidy. No sign of a struggle, no hoards of papers or half eaten sandwiches. The radio was on, which I found a good sign. I called out but there was no answer.

Ill? I said.

Gone. Rockwell said. Vanished, disappeared - just not there. I searched everywhere hoping after the first half hour to find a trace, a body even, but there was nothing.

I let my cousin in and we went through that house, room by room. It has three bedrooms and a large kitchen, plus a very airy front room. Quite comfortable and worth a pretty penny, if you are of a mind to sell. Well as I said, Rockwell came in close,

Nothing at all - except...

Except?

A will written in his own hand and a diary.

Oh.

And two of the strangest things. In Lionel's front room with his book and pipe, in his favourite comfy chair and the radio on, was...

Yes?

A cockroach.

And the second thing?

In Lionel's bed was another roach, on his pillow, sleeping.

Mr Rockwell sighed and folded his arms across his chest.

It was only when we read the diary that all that had gone before was revealed. And the last entry said Lionel wanted to leave all his worldly possessions to the cockroach. Everything.

And your uncle wasn't to be found anywhere?

Mr Rockwell shrugged his shoulders. He looked around the shop and when satisfied it was still empty he asked in a low voice,

Have you read Kafka Mr Weatherness?

I pondered the question when Mr Rockwell produced several sheets of paper. So the question I wanted to ask your advice about was this.

Can I claim poor Uncle Lionel's will? After all, a cockroach cannot be entitled - can they?

Plate VIII

Seymour Ham.

They say lightning never strikes twice in the same place. The person that said this has never been to the Cape. Cape York at the tip of the continent is renowned for lightning.

I was on my way to Thursday Island on the new airline service from Cairns, when we were grounded because of a storm. I had travelled by boat to this remote outpost once or twice and seen what Mother Nature could throw at the unwary traveller, so was quite willing to wait. I sat back in the lounge and closed my eyes when a voice to my right made me sit up.
I don't care how long it takes.

The passenger was a middle aged man with a furrowed brow. He was wearing a well worn suit and had his hat on his knee. He leant forward in his seat and perched his elbows on his knees, holding his head in his hands. He seemed to have the weight of the world on his shoulders. He sighed and ran his fingers though his thick dark hair.

Shall we have a cup of tea to pass the time? I asked. He said he'd rather something stronger and so we walked to the bar. With a beer in his hand he brightened up a little and introduced himself. Seymour Ham, he said, holding out his hand. I shook it.

Trododniak Weatherness.

He looked at me and frowned.

A family tradition, I explained. Mr Ham nodded and then started to talk.

I suppose you are wondering why I don't want to get back to the Island. I sipped my beer and shrugged my shoulders. Well, I will tell you why and then you'll see I'm justified, he said. We took our drinks to the comfy chairs and sat down.

My life was pretty predictable. I was born in Melbourne, went to school with average grades and finished in a fine job with an insurance company. I am an actuary.

Mr Ham looked at me for a moment of understanding. I nodded that I knew what his job might entail.

Things were on the up an' up for me. Then I met Kate. She made my life complete.

Mr Ham fished about in his coat pocket and came up with his wallet. He flipped it open and showed me a picture of a petite woman squinting into the sun. She was laughing and had her hand shading her eyes and her arm around an Islander woman's shoulder. The picture was taken at a beach, probably on holiday and gave the feeling of happiness.

A handsome woman, I said. Mr Ham nodded and sighed, gazing at the photograph.

Kate was everything I had hoped for in life. Pretty, smart, homely and happy. What more could a man want. What are the odds of striking the jackpot first time?

I smiled.

We set up house in the suburbs of Melbourne, took out a small mortgage and began to think of a family. I would go to work every day knowing I would be coming home to comfort and dependability. It was all just wonderful.

You're a lucky man, I said.

You'd think so wouldn't you, he replied. He leaned back in his seat and seemed to me to be gathering courage to go on.

So we decided that it was time to add to our happiness. I had a promotion, the house payments were ticking along and I calculated the next three years of our lives would be the ideal time to start a family.

Around this time I was asked to go away on a trip. The company needed a senior man on the ground. They asked me to go to Thursday Island and look over the viability of a business. It was an opportunity to negotiate a big deal for the company. They promised great things if I could pull it off. Who wouldn't do it? From the bottom of Australia to the top. I'd never been further than Canberra so you can imagine I was excited and I had gone over the likely-hood of success and the figures seemed good.

Kate and I had never been apart for a long period of time. It was to be our first separation. We had only been married for a year.

Mr Ham looked at me and asked,

Are you married? I said my wife had died a long time ago. He nodded and continued.

Our separation would only strengthen our love. Absence make the heart grow fonder they say, he smiled. I promised to write, telephone when I could and to miss her dreadfully. She promised the same.

The trip up north was to be broken by work along the way. I had to stop in some of our regional offices and attend to a few outstanding matters. I would be away for two months.

I wrote twice a week and Kate wrote via the next office I would be visiting.

Seymour looked out of the large window at the airfield. We watched a pilot hold onto his hat as the wind tried to take it and struggle to walk to the building. He reached the door and wrenched it open against the wind then stumbled inside.

We both heard the word 'cyclone', as he disappeared with some staff into another room.

It looks like we will be here for quite a while, I said. Mr Ham nodded.

So I finally came to Cairns to catch the boat, Elsana to Thursday Island.

Have you been on that trip?
I have, I said. Several times.
Then you know what it is to be sea sick.
Yes.
I had never been on a boat before. It was awful. I was ill. Very ill.
I knew just what Seymour meant. I had only once been taken by sea sickness. At the time if someone had given me a gun, I just might have used it.

I stayed in my room most of the trip, but then I thought I needed air. I didn't know where we were, how far from land, how near to the Island, but I didn't care. All I felt was that I needed air. So I went up on deck in the storm. Wild men couldn't have kept me from fresh air. I watched as Mr Ham's eyes widened.
And that's when it happened.
What?
I staggered up on the deck and had just stepped out and BAM! I was struck by lightning.
My word, I exclaimed.
Too right, Ham said. He turned his head and showed me a scar behind his ear extending down under his collar.
Just like that! He snapped his fingers. What are the odds? What are the chances of that?
Low I would assume, I answered.
Exactly, one in 1.6 million. Seymour Ham, I thought to myself, lived and breathed actuary acumen.

Of course I collapsed. You don't get 1 billion volts and still be able to tie your shoelaces.

The Captain told me I was lucky. Can you believe it? He said, because I was holding onto the steel door handle the electricity travelled through me to the boat and the sea.

Well, I was out to it, they tell me, for one whole day. Seymour Ham looked at me with an uncomfortable stare.

Imagine. Losing one day of your life. No recollections, no memories for one whole day.

Mmmm, I mused.

Well...when I came around I had lost more than that. I was a different person. I couldn't remember who I was, where I belonged, what past I had had. The Captain explained who Seymour Ham was, what he was doing, where he was supposed to be, but it was all news to me.

Amnesia? I said.

I didn't trust anyone. I thought they were trying to trick me and so I locked myself in my room for the remainder of the voyage. When we arrived at the Island I just about ran off that boat and vowed never to travel with rogues like that again. He stopped talking and we sipped our drinks.

And then the strangest thing happened. I looked around and it all felt familiar. Don't ask me how. It felt like I was coming home.

Can you believe that? Ham asked. I shook my head.

Well I walked up the main street and people started to say hello like they knew me. I didn't know what was going on, I can tell you. Then a woman came up and asked me where I had been.

Ham looked at me,

She just threaded her arm in mine and kissed me on the cheek. She was so happy to see me. I was shocked. So I disengaged her grip and took a good look at this woman. There was no doubt she was good looking. Very pretty, young. An Islander girl no more than 25 years old.

Look, I said, I don't know you and if this is a joke it is not very funny. Well the Captain was walking by just then and he explained to her that I had been struck by lightning and probably just needed to go home, to rest.

Home? I asked. I knew I lived in Melbourne. Home, the young woman said and she led me to a smart little house and you won't believe it, but it also looked familiar.

There was no doubt I was confused and so I asked her.

Asked what? I said.

Who was she and what was all this about.

And what did she say?

She said I was her husband.

Can you believe it?

I don't understand? I said to Ham.

Neither did I Mr Weatherness.

So I told her I was married to Kate, in Melbourne and she must have the wrong man. It was then she showed me the wedding photo. There I was in a suit, smiling, standing next to her in her wedding dress. It was impossible, but true. I just sort of collapsed and when I came around there was the Island doctor in attendance.

And what was the diagnosis?

He said he had known me for three years. I had been married for three years to this woman and then he explained what might have happened. I can tell you it was a strange story.

Three years ago I came to the island by boat. I was ill and the doctor brought me back to health.

Nothing too serious? I said.

You won't believe it. I was struck by lightning.

My goodness, I exclaimed.

Exactly.

The doctor said that I was lucky to be alive. He said I had come to do some work for a big company on the mainland, but considering my condition they relieved me of the work until I was fully recuperated. Marni, the young woman, looked after me and I fell in love with my nurse. It was love on both sides, apparently.

Seymour turned to gaze out the window.

She was very pretty, he said.

So when I was well we decided to get married. We set up house and I worked as the Island agent and life was good. Then about the three year mark I went to the mainland and just didn't come back. They thought I had run away. Not everyone is cut out to Island life. And a white man marrying a Islander, well, Mr Weatherness, you understand the complexities.

I'm not one to shirk my responsibilities, Mr Weatherness, but something must have happened. Ham pointed to his head, up here, he said.

So now I had apparently come home and as I had been struck for the second time my mind was in a jumble. The doctor gave me some pills and soon I just sort of accepted what these people were telling me. I gradually realized I belonged, settled down and felt happy...for a while.
Oh, I said.
Gradually I began to remember. Dreams at first, then more like nightmares. I came to realise I had two wives. I knew my dreams were real. I had a mortgage, a house and another life.
What is a bloke supposed to do with two wives? Ham ran his fingers through his hair in a nervous fashion.
I shook my head.
I didn't want to say anything to Marni, my life was good on the Island, but of course I felt guilty, very guilty, because I knew Kate was in Melbourne waiting for me.
So what did you do? I was curious.
Nothing.
Nothing? I said.
How could I? Marni was in love with me and I was married. She was happy. I figured that I had been married to her longer than Kate and so she had first priority. Then...
Yes?

Then I received a letter. It was postmarked from Melbourne and I knew. I knew it was from Kate. So I opened it and it put my mind in turmoil. She was coming to the Island. Now I had to do something.

What did the letter say? I knew my inquiry was presumptuous, but I was intrigued.

You wanna drink? Seymour asked. I said yes.

Ham went for our drinks and then when settled in his seat, again he continued.

Kate had always been a go getter type of girl. She was always lively and up for it, whatever *it* would be. That's why I liked her I guess. Well, she said she had searched for me and eventually someone had said I was on T.I. If I was in her position I would want to know. It's only natural, Ham said.

Yes, I guess I would be the same, I said.

So I had to tell Marni. It wasn't easy.

And how did she react?

She said she would meet Kate and they would work it out. I could only hope they would sort it out, because I didn't have any idea how it would end, besides me going to gaol for bigamy.

Kate came by plane. A much safer option if you ask me. Seymour looked out the window at the darkening sky. I followed his gaze and we watched a tree struggle to hold onto the earth as the wind tried to tear its grip.

I met her on the dock because the plane lands at Horn Island and you have to take a boat. She stepped off and when I saw her again I knew I loved her more than ever. She was my Kate. Marni was there too and I introduced the two women in my life. Kate seemed to be a good sport about it and we all went home.

Ham faced me. You know the old tribal chiefs often had more than one wife. I began to think we could all live together, you know, as a family. I think I was dreaming.

So?

So we sort of all stayed in the one house and then something happened. Marni and Kate began to be friends. They would talk, joke and laugh, usually at my expense, but they just seemed to get on.

That must have been a relief for you.

You'd think? Ham said.

I was earning decent wage. A very good wage and so I thought if Kate wanted to stay we could set up another house next to mine and she might try to be happy on the Island.

It was a daring experiment?

You don't have to tell me. But Kate said she'd go for it.

We sold the Melbourne house and built a lovely bungalow for her, right next door. It *was* a very good arrangement.

Was? I asked.

As a married man, you must know what women are like.

I nodded in understanding.

Well we all just mucked in and go on, if you can imagine. I had the two loves of my life and everyone was happy, then things started to change. It just sort of crept up on me. First Kate would say things like, Marni really needs a new table, or Marni's having trouble with her plumbing. I'd jump right on it and thought it was just like Kate to be generous and helpful. Then Marni might say Kate wants her vegie patch dug, or Kate could do with a new cupboard. Marni was always helping people, it's in her nature.

I still had to work, but the women wanted me to do things for them all the time. It became a bit of a bone.

I nodded and sipped my drink.

I tried to do my best, but it seemed my best wasn't good enough. Ham once again held his head in his hands with his elbows on his knees.

Why do women change?

It was a question I couldn't answer.

Kate and Marni were beautiful, young, lively and fun. Then they became shrews.

Oh. I said.

Soon it was, Seymour do this, Seymour do that. Nothing was ever right or good enough. The women I had married became united in their nagging. They were best friends. I was the target of their insistent haranguing. It didn't end there either.

They joined the houses and lived in the biggest house on the Island. My 'luck', as some would have it, was to have two beautiful women in the same house.

It wasn't luck.

Oh. I sat back and folded my hands on my lap.

Not lucky at all. I spent all my days and nights trying to please them. And they were never pleased. The only pleasure, it seemed to me, that they derived, was nagging me. They would spend hours talking to one another, probably scheming up ways to get at me.

So I did what any man would do.

What's that?

I tried to stay away. I went on business trips. I went on fishing expeditions. I made excuses to travel.

Of course I had an obligation to help with the financial side of things. They were my wives after all. I didn't stint on that. But as for sharing a life with them I'd rather choke on a boiled egg.

We looked at the weather when there was an announcement over the tannoy. Due to the worsening conditions our flight had been cancelled until further notice.

Seymour Ham breathed a sigh of relief.

Sometimes, he said, I wish I could get struck by lightning...again. What are the odds of that?

Plate IX

    Miss Willmott & Mr Crick.

    Sometimes the only way to get a feel for a small town is to visit the local museum. Most towns have one and it is here you see what has made the place, what binds the fabric of the community together.
    Magnetic Island just off the coast of Townsville has a village feel to the place. People have been coming to the Island for pleasure for many years. The Butler family carved out a tourist niche and jealously guarded their patch.
    I happened upon the museum in Picnic Bay on Magnetic Island and read all about the Butlers and the Chinese market gardens and spent a good enjoyable hour or so looking at the photographic history and a marvellous collection of insects.

Miss Willmott was a stout woman in the photograph. Her eyes were small and black as boot buttons and yet even with a scowl and pursed lips I could sense something more in the woman. A feeling that she had never quite let herself go or had done anything other than what was required. She was dressed in a drab dark coloured dress, clutching a shawl across her breast like a shield against the world. Her hair was pulled back, in a bun I presumed and not a stray hair out of place. Her picture hung in the local museum with just her name by way of introduction. Miss Willmott's hands were held tight to her shawl and no wedding band adorned the ring finger, no bracelet encircled the wrist and no watch kept the moment fresh. She was plain, unadorned and I could not stop looking at her. It was only later in the tea rooms on the foreshore promenade that I heard the full story of Miss Willmott and by association, Mr Crick.

In search of a cup of tea I was directed by a local to the only tea room in Picnic Bay. Nestled between a fishing tackle shop and a hairdressers it had a faded billboard out the front and about half a dozen tables inside, all empty. The bell on the door indicated my presence and I sat down at a window seat. A sturdy looking woman came out from the back and smoothed her apron down, looked me over and when satisfied with her appraisal asked me for my order. With the business out the way I gazed out of the window at the dirty looking sea foaming to the sandy shore.

Looks like a bit of a chop coming in, the woman said then introduced herself. Mrs Blane, this is my shop.

Nothing like a cup of tea, I offered to the conversation.

Yes. You on holiday? Mrs Blane asked.

Well, yes and no. A small matter to attend to and then I'm free for a day or so.

Plenty to see on the Island if you like walking, she said and left to get my order. The sea did look choppy as I watched the ferry leave for the mainland. I felt a small surge of isolation watching the ferry depart. I have found island life brings a sense on introspection as the mainland is another world away. Mrs Blane came back presently with my pot of tea and stood at the window,

A Northerly coming in, she said.

Is that bad?

Not particularly. Happens this time of year. Cleveland Bay is a shallow nasty piece of water whatever the weather. She studied the weather then said,

Been to the museum?

Yes, I said. I spent a good hour there. Very interesting. There is more to the Island than I realised. Quite a potted history.

Mmm, Mrs Blane mused and picked at a stray hair over her face.

I saw one photo. A woman, I said. Do you know anything about a Miss Willmott? I saw her picture and there was something about her that pricked my curiosity. Such a concentrated stare. Mrs Blane folded her arms across her large breasts and looked at me.

Miss Willmott you say?

Yes. Just something about the picture that was a little unnerving, I said.

I can tell you about Miss Willmott, if you like. I nodded and poured myself a cup of tea. Mrs Blane stood with her back to the window and smiled at me and began to talk.

Miss Willmott's life, it seemed, was not a happy one. Her claim to fame to be in the local museum was linked to her charitable nature and a sizable donation towards the war memorial in the park. I had passed the memorial earlier on my walk and nodded in recognition.

Elsie Willmott was an only child. A surprise late in life to her parents, she grew up with none of the gaiety of siblings, none of the spontaneity of young parents and consequently she was middle aged by the time she turned 21.

Her beauty was within, the pastor used to say when Elsie sat with her parents in church. The girl must have some talents, her teachers would tell her parents adding; we just haven't found them yet. To Elsie, the world was something to be endured, something to be got through, like a chilblain or a bad cold. Mr and Mrs Willmott it can be said, tried their best, but with little to go by in the way of experience, as they both were only children, they fed Elsie, they clothed Elsie and they took her to church on Sunday, but that was about the sum of their love. The Willmott household was rooted in routine and Elsie was governed by the clock, the seasons, and the opening times at the library.

It was said, Miss Willmott was the libraries best customer and as the township consisted, in a good fishing season of around sixty souls, their only customer.

Mrs Blane, the tea room proprietor in Picnic Bay explained her intimate knowledge of Miss Willmott.
My cousin lived next door to the Willmott house. It's empty now, has been for many years. In a small hamlet this was enough of a connection.

Elsie Willmott, when of age, fell into the job of librarian. The library was really just a small room off the school house, but the shire council had budgeted for the civic amenity and although the wage was meagre, it was enough. Later when the population increased it had a staff of three, but when Miss Willmott was in control it was small. The library was Miss Willmott's life.

Do you read? Mrs Blane asked me. I nodded,
Yes.
Well, Miss Willmott read everything. She started at A and didn't stop until she reached Zola. It was a great education to her, but her fancy was romance. She seemed to live for the books and while she was reading her romances, the real world passed her by. Children were born, schooled and moved away. Contemporaries were married and raising families and all the while Miss Willmott looked after her books. She didn't seem to mind. She seemed happy enough in her own world and life went on in Picnic Bay.

Mind you, Mrs Blane said, this all happened quite a while ago. Just before and after the Great War. The date confirmed my suspicions, as I had guessed the period when looking at the photographs.

Mrs Blane looked out the window at the choppy sea, then as the tea room was empty, she offered to refresh my pot.

We get a lot of day trippers. Visitors like to come here for the island life, Mrs Blane said as she pulled up a chair at my table. The place used to hum with all sorts of people, and still does when it's hot on the mainland. Mrs Blane fiddled with the cruet set.

Well one summer it was particularly hot. The temperature soared and the ferry was full of trippers trying to get relief. A sea breeze is worth anything when you're hot. But this wasn't the reason for a gentleman called, Mr Crick coming to the Island. He had an appointment with Miss Willmott.

Mr Crick was a keen collector of insects.

Bugs, Mrs Blane explained giving a shudder. He had heard of the small Picnic Bay library and on the off chance of an out of date copy of an insect compendium, he had written to Miss Willmott and received a reply. The library had a little sale once a year for volumes that were old, dog eared or hadn't been borrowed and were unpopular. Miss Willmott indicated that Mr Crick might be in luck if he was interested in buying the book. It was enough of a promise for the man to make the journey.

Day trippers are a casual lot, Mrs Blane said. They strut around in shirt sleeves, the women in sun dresses and sandals and never a hat to be seen. I've seen women in shorts like it's Hollywood or something.

Mrs Blane had firm ideas on what was acceptable and what was not.

In Miss Willmott's era it would have been the same as people just let their hair down a little when on the Island. Mr Crick was made of sterner stuff. In a time when propriety was all the rage Mr Crick was steadfast in his adherence. Although it was hot the day he came, his hat and coat remained in place and by the time he arrived at the small wooden annex which was the library, he was a bath of perspiration.

Mrs Blane told the story as if she was an eye witness. I sat back and enjoyed the drama of the telling as she continued.

The room was ventilated and well shaded by a mango tree and a welcome relief from the sun. The mango tree is still there if you care to look. Some things never change, she said.

Mr Crick entered to see a composed, demure woman sitting at a table, working.

Mrs Blane smoothed out the table cloth and sat back to look me in the eye.

Some say it was love at first sight, but I think it took a little longer.

Miss Willmott, seeing the man suffering, offered him a drink from the canvas bag hanging under the window. She had delicate hands, never having to worry about the chores of a wife and mother and Mr Crick was struck by her genteel manner. Men of Mr Crick's nature were few and far between in the library and Miss Willmott was quite taken by this gentleman. The most she had seen of gentlemanly behaviour was the minister and he lapsed on the communion wine quite often.

How old was Miss Willmott? I asked.
She was a spinster of 40. The word spinster was placed with some emphasis and I guessed Mrs Blane was one of life's well and truly married women.

The transaction was completed and Mr Crick had no reason to stay, but stay he did. He talked of his hobby, his work in the army, his life and all the while Miss Willmott listened. Her life was highlighted by a bottle of champagne when she was 21. Mr Crick seemed exotic.

Mr Crick took the last ferry of the afternoon and there was a vague promise of correspondence if a slim volume on spiders could be found.

Miss Willmott now had a quest. She hunted, she wrote letters and she secured the book and summoned Mr Crick.

His next visit was on a wintery day, the seas menacing and threatening to close the ferry service, but he endured the sea sickness to see Miss Willmott. The meeting was cordial and to Mr Crick's surprise Miss Willmott had started to take an interest in bug. She had also laid out an afternoon tea.

I guess all those books on romance had fuelled her desires, Mrs Blane looked at me.

Are you married? She asked.

I nodded. My wife died many years ago, I said.

Desire is one thing, 8 children is another, Mrs Blane said as she twisted her wedding band around her finger. They spent an afternoon together all the while keeping up appearances.

Times change don't they? Mrs Blane began. These days the young people just share a milk shake and they are kissing. I blame all those Hollywood films. They fill the heads of young people with all manner of notions about love. I surmised Mrs Blane had a particular bone to pick about the morals of Hollywood. She flicked a sugar crystal from the table cloth to the floor and went on.

Mr Crick visited the island several times after that, always in the pursuit of a bug book. Miss Willmott always managed to secure the book he had in mind. It was a partnership.

And they fell in love? I said.

Well...Mrs Blane smiled.

To the others in Picnic Bay it was purely a commercial arrangement. No-one saw anything more as they conducted themselves with solemn manners. It was always Miss Willmott and Mr Crick. There wasn't a hint of romance about their dealings. Nothing that could be considered romantic. Nothing like the books Miss Willmott read with such delight. Letters and parcels went through the post office, books were exchanged and the bay thought nothing of it. This went on for some time and when things happen regularly they become the ordinary. That's how it was.

Then Miss Willmott's parents needed care. They were elderly and what could a dutiful daughter do? Miss Willmott took on the task. She *was* a dutiful daughter, and they lived a good ten years longer than expected with her care. She was selfless in her devotion right up to the end. Mr Willmott went first and it often happens that the other partner pines and it wasn't 5 months when Mrs Willmott went next to her husband in the cemetery.

In the meantime Mr Crick went away to the Great War. It was a time of sacrifice all 'round. Mr Crick was away for the duration. Being an army man, when the war ended he still had a job to do, but as he had had a dose of gas, his career was over. Then not long after he came back to Queensland, he died. Three tragedies within the space of one year. Anyone would seem ragged after that. Miss Willmott was no exception, although people didn't see it. She just carried on as usual and life went on around her. She was such a fixture that people just didn't see what was under their noses.

Mrs Blane sighed and sat back in her chair.

It wasn't long after Mr Crick's death when one day the library didn't open. Miss Willmott had never missed a day. She wasn't the type of person to just take a holiday and so the residents of Picnic Bay began to become anxious. Miss Willmott was a stalwart character. No-one wants to pry, but in a small community there is a feeling of family. Someone went around to the Willmott house and she wasn't there. They knew she couldn't have taken the ferry, someone would have seen her. So a search party was called for and they scoured the island. Horses trekked up to the summit. People combed the road and verge. They brought over the police from the mainland and went from Horseshoe Bay right through Florence, Radical to Picnic. Boats were called for and went right around the Island. The search was in the papers. It was a big effort and involved just about every islander. That first day there was nothing.

And? I looked at the sea from my window seat.

She had thrown herself off the rocks.

Mrs Blane pointed to an outcrop of rocks at the end of the bay.

They found her the next day.

Mrs Blane sighed. It is the only suicide on the Island. No-one before, no-one since.

So the authorities went around to the Willmott family home. Trying to find some answers, to make sense of the thing.

And what did they find? I sat forward in anticipation.

Letters. Hundreds of letters. And books on bugs.

Miss Willmott and Mr Crick had been in love. Desperately in love.

Their letters contained poems of love. Declarations of devotion and quotations from

Shakespeare. For 20 years they had loved one another. His letters were startling in their tenderness. Her letters were full of the romance of love. It was a classic love story.

Mrs Blane picked at the tablecloth.

And there were bugs. Bugs of all description in small cases with neat handwritten descriptions. They shared a passion of love and of insects.

So what kept them apart? I inquired.

Duty. It had to be duty.

Miss Willmott had a duty to her parents. Mr Crick had a duty to country. Neither could cross the line to think of themselves. But when Mr Crick died, Miss Willmott could bare it no more and she threw her life away.

There is a bug apparently, Mrs Blane said, that only loves once, then dies.

I drained the last of my tea and Mrs Blane looked at the empty cup.

It was discovered that she had saved a sizable fortune. Her will stipulated money for the war memorial. Her book collection on bugs was to go to the library, and the insects themselves to the museum.

She looked so stern in the photograph I saw at the museum, I said.

Stern or unhappy? It is a fine line.

We looked out the window at the gathering clouds.

Mrs Blane followed me to the door and on seeing a Rhinoceros beetle on the step kicked it away with her foot.

Bug, she said and shuddered.

Plate X

Edward Addison

I have never been one to lose things. I like to know where things are and relish order over chaos. But on a particularly windy night in Barcaldine, after I had left the pub, I realised I had left my hat behind at the Artesian Hotel. I didn't expect it to be stolen, the population of township was quite small albeit with a grand history behind it. The focal point of Barcaldine being the 'tree of knowledge' and its part in the birth of the Australian Labour Party. I could have retrieved it in the morning, but felt I needed to get it immediately, probably my neat and tidy nature coming to the fore, so I trudged back to the pub just on closing time and found it on the peg where I had parked it.

Lucky I remembered it, I said to the publican. The landlord nodded in my direction and held up a whisky bottle.

One for the road, he offered. I consented.

Just one, I said, and sat down as he closed the doors behind me. It was a lock-in and I knew from experience, the drinking could go on for some while.

Manson, the publican introduced himself. Jim Manson. He was a thick set fellow with just the whisper of hair on his head. His beard made up for any shortfall. It was a voluminous affair peppered with white and covered the top two buttons of his shirt. Manson seemed to be well suited to his job with meaty hands and a no-nonsense look about him. He produced two glasses and put them on the bar then poured a good measure of Irish whisky in each and looked at my hat.

Do you believe in luck sir? He asked.

I shook my head. I hadn't seen too much luck in my profession as a Magistrate.

Well, he started, I will tell you a story about luck and you just might change your mind. Manson slugged back his whisky, I sipped mine and he began.

The purchase of a hat is a personal thing. There is much that goes into the choice, besides the size. It says who you are to the world, what your character is and how you want to be known.

Manson looked at my hat resting on the bar stool next to me. I had bought it in Brisbane and fancied it suited me well.

Edward Addison wore a bushman's hat. Nothing fancy, but with a wide brim and a leather band. He didn't care for the flash, the fashionable and that hat had served him well. He was a stocky fellow with a mop of dark hair and tanned face that was pleasing on the eye plus a broad smile. He stood just under a soldier's height, but with square strong shoulders he looked a lot taller. He was honest, trustworthy and hardworking. The qualities that country folk are brought up with, and carry throughout their whole lives. His family have been around these parts for years. Addison was brought up on the land and it was in his blood. He had two brothers, but they didn't love the land like Edward.

Manson reached for the bottle and poured another.

You want one?

I shook my head and held my hand over my glass.

You either got the land in your veins or you haven't.

It was Addison's habit to take a drink once a week on a Friday night. He was a beer man and his habit was a regular as clockwork. A more steady fellow you couldn't meet. Content with his life, content with his lot. Well one Friday he didn't show.

Manson and raised his eye brows.

In a small town like Barcaldine, he said, your business is everybody's business. The highway may bring in newcomers, but it just as easily takes them away. Edward Addison didn't show because he had lost his job. He was a farm hand and the drought had brought the industry to its knees. It's a crime to see the cattle starving, the land being taken over by prickles and not a God damn thing you can do about it. Our district is too far away from the big towns, for those that tough it out here, to just move to other jobs, but not far enough to be immune from the world. Some go to Emerald, but most just scratch a living between the lagoon and the cemetery. With a wife and child to support things were looking grim for Addison. There were stories like this all over the district and as a town we did what we could, but belts were tight all around. So one Wednesday, Edward came into the pub and said he was having his last pleasure. His last drink before the family had to move away. It was a sobering time as we all knew his circumstances might very well be our own. There was a whip 'round and Addison knew who his friends were that day.

It was a touching story and I nodded at the all too familiar tale.

So Edward left to a few pats on the back, a few well wishes and a couple of good lucks. Except when he went to collect his hat it was gone. It was almost the last straw for Edward and in a fit of temper he grabbed the first hat he saw, shoved it on his head and walked out.

I looked at my own hat sitting on the stool next to me.

Now you'd think the owner of that hat would come forward, but no-one did. Edward went home and slept it off. Then the very next day he was sent a message from his previous employer. Turns out the Dickenson place where he worked had found some water underground. So, Edward could have his job back, things weren't so grim and for good measure he'd be promoted to foreman with extra pay.

It was cause for celebration in the Addison household that night.

Manson lit a cigarette and I followed his lead and we shared a match.

So with a change of luck Addison felt quite chipper and he began coming into town on a Friday like usual. Things just pegged along for a time then one Friday he bought a lottery ticket from the local women's guild. The prize was a trip to the big smoke by train, a hotel room and a swanky restaurant meal. The funds were for the local health centre.

And he won? I asked.

Yep. First bloody prize. Now Addison, for a fact, had never won anything in his life. Not a thing, but ever since he had been wearing that Fedora things had changed.

I frowned at the assumption. Manson looked me in the eye.

Well that was his take on his turn of fortune anyway.

Edward had had a nagging pain in his back for years. He fell off a horse once as a youngster and landed badly, but he was never one to complain or ask for favours. He just got on the with job, we all do, don't we? Well he came into town one Friday and instead of easing himself onto a stool or standing as is his normal way he just plopped himself down and smiled at me. I was a bit surprised, cause I'd seen him wincing in pain on more than one occasion, so I asked him what happened.

Now, he said, the pain had gone. Disappeared. He felt vital and fit. It was more than just medical management; it was luck. How could it be anything else, he said.

Then he came into the pub one Friday just after the rodeo had been though and announced that his hat was his lucky hat. A smooth finish brown fur felt, brim 2 3/4" bound edge, back teardrop crown with a crossgrain 1" band, with satin lining and an inside leather sweatband. We drank to his good luck and said if ever a man deserved a little luck it was Addison.

I, as much as the next man, like to see someone get a little of what they deserve. There was no doubting that Edward's life was coming good. The family didn't have that hang dog look anymore and Addison; well he was a happy man.

The lottery trip to the city was an eye opener for that family and they saw the things money could buy. Mrs Addison said they should capitalize on their fortunate turn of events and it wasn't long before they had spread his wages over several of the shopping catalogues in the pursuit of happiness. Mrs Addison was an ordinary woman. She didn't have a glamorous look or anything. She wasn't ugly either, just run of the mill. A bit on the skinny side, but then, isn't everyone these days with the war and all. Anyway the Addison family were getting along with their little bit of luck when, as luck would have it, some land came on the market. There wasn't keen interest in the estate as it was considered barren, dry and almost worthless. But Addison saw that little bit of Queensland as an investment. He had never had the opportunity to own land and thought with good husbandry, management and hard work they just might turn it around into something worth having.

We have more than our fair share of scrub this way. The land can look inviting, but it is only the snakes and the hawks that have an advantage. If you want to make a living you need water. It's just a fact of life. Without water all you have is dirt.

I nodded. I had seen the landscape as I had arrived and with the the only green the scrubby little trees trying to suck life from the dust, and the grey-red earth parched of any goodness, it seemed another God forsaken place on this earth.

The auction was well attended, Manson gave me a wry smile.

Not much happens out here and any excuse to get together is good enough. The Hartley acreage, with its broken fences, dry bore and weed infested pasture didn't exactly attract a bidding war. Mrs Addison wasn't for it at all, but Edward wanted something he could call his own.

A man needs something he can call his own. It makes all the difference when at the end of a hard day you can sit back and look out from the verandah and know you own all you can see.

Did he succeed? I asked. Manson nodded.

A guinea.

A bargain, I said.

So you'd think, Manson said then added, I'll get to that in a moment.

With the feeling of success Mrs Addison said he should buy a lottery ticket. She was always trying to capitalise on their good fortune. Trying to squeeze that little bit extra. Although she wasn't keen on the Hartley place, she reckoned she could be rid of it in a year or two and with their luck make a small profit.

He won?

Yep. £8,000. It was the most anyone had ever dreamed of in the way of money in Barcaldine. His wife said it was because of the hat. Everything that had happened was because of that hat. She guarded that hat jealously. She nagged Edward to wear it, never to lose it, to keep it safe. And he did, but things changed. He didn't seem the same man. He didn't look happy.

Previous to the hat he was a contented man. He gave to the community. He had a place in the town and his expectations were like every other mans. Now he was different. Things fell in his lap. His wife always wanted more. She was never satisfied as before. And the bone that stuck in her throat the most was the Hartley land. Oh how she hated that land. It was a millstone, worthless, a drain on their energies she would say. She wanted to be rid of it, but Edward said no. She threatened to leave him if he didn't sell, but he knew she wouldn't. She had too much to lose, with his good luck never ending. Addison invested his winnings and made more money. But for every pound he made, he became morose, and his wife nagged him even more. He won the sweepstakes. He won the raffle. His wife, the most bejewelled, his son the best dressed, but all this was like a dead weight to him. His friends drifted away, his company was never sought and he drank at home, alone - with his hat.

Manson stubbed out his cigarette.
The moral of the tale I expect, I inquired. Manson wagged his second cigarette at me.
Well...of sorts. Addison began to hate that hat. His wife never stopped nagging him about it. He blamed all his woes on that hat so the obvious thing would be to get rid of it. He had enough money to last. He had his land, his job, his health. All that was missing was happiness and that was down to the hat.

I ask you, can a man have too much luck?
Perhaps ones expectations change with ones fortunes, I said.
Could be. Manson answered. He studied the ashtray and sighed.

So one Friday he came into the pub and left the hat on the stand. Manson pointed to the hat stand where I had left my hat earlier. He stayed late, drank too much and when he went to leave his hat was waiting for him. So he came in the next night and the next, but his hat was always on the peg where he left it. So he went home without it. And someone returned it. He sat it on a fence post and it blew into his yard. And all the while his wife berated him.

Things carried on like that for a bit, then one Friday night he came in for a drink and made it a few. He was well on his way to being thrown out when an old codger came in looking for work, down on his luck. I usually give them a feed and let them work it off in the yard. We all have to do our little bit.

An admirable sentiment, I said.

Edward looked at the fellow and must have recognised himself not so long ago and so gave him some charity. It was the first decent thing he had done in a long time and it made him feel good. The bloke said he'd work for it and then Edward sent him to his piece of land to fix a gate.

A man needs honest work. Charity is all very well, and serves its purpose, but work builds a man's self worth. Don't you think? Manson asked.

Yes, of course, I replied.

So, now Edward was feeling pretty good and it seemed to him he needed to repeat the exercise and the next thing he did was to give a sizable chunk of his good fortune to the church, then the women's guild. And you know what? His happiness increased. But the down side, and there is always a down side, was that the more he gave away the more shrew-like his wife became. She became the bane of his existence.

Nagging about this or that. Following him into town to have a go at him in the bar. No woman comes into my bar and I had to ask her to leave more than once. Women have their place and it's not in the front bar of the Artesian Hotel on a Friday evening. What can a man do with a wife like that? I tell you, Edward had given her everything. The woman should have been in clover, but she wasn't. All you can do is get away.

He took himself to the Hartley land looking for satisfaction in honest labour and hard work. And if the truth be known to get away from Mrs Addison.

Did he find it? I said.

Yup.

Manson corked the whisky and stubbed out his cigarette.

So all it took was for him to see luck isn't material wealth, it is more ephemeral than that. Manson looked at me and smiled.

So one Friday evening, Edward walked into the pub, parked his fedora on the hat stand and said drinks all round. I asked him, what was the occasion? He said that he had found an artesian basin of water on the Hartley property. It would be barren no more. We toasted his good luck, when someone at the bar said his misses would be pleased 'cause we all knew she thought it was the worst decision Edward had ever made. Edward turned to the man and said she was the one that found it. She fell down a hole and he didn't hear her hit the bottom.

By luck or design? I said.

The publican sucked on his front teeth and picked up his rag and began to wipe the bar.

You could have heard a pin drop. Edward finished his drink and walked out - without his hat.

There was talk of a fellow who passed this way. Found a gem the size of a shilling near Emerald. Someone said he was wearing a fedora. Manson looked at me.

It can happen like that. I stood up and went to pay.

On the house, Manson said.

I grabbed my hat and once outside put it on against the wind. It didn't feel quite right and I adjusted it several times then took it off to have a closer look under the street lamp.

A smooth finish brown fur felt, brim 2 3/4" bound edge, back teardrop crown with a crossgrain 1" band, with satin lining and an inside leather sweatband. I put it on again and felt my luck about to change.

Plate XI

Dolly & Harold Lancome

I went up on deck for a smoke before the cargo ship, Arc Julius departed and stood on the port side idly gazing at the hub of activity on the dock. Presently a cab pulled up and I watched a middle aged couple step out and casually walk to the gang plank; like they had all the time in the world. If they had heard the Captain swearing an hour earlier they might have quickened their pace.

He was a serious looking fellow rugged up with a coat and scarf although the weather was mild. She on the other hand was in a spring dress which, caught by the wind, was flattened onto her middle aged body with all its inherent flaws. She held onto her hat, a frilly thing with flowers and bows and tried to control her dress with her other hand while laughing. It was a laugh of carefree abandon and little did I know how that laugh would grate on my nerves by the third day of the twenty one day voyage.

The woman began to direct traffic, instructing the man, her husband I guessed, to gather the luggage, pay the driver, instruct the porters and deckhands and by the look of it keep the gathering clouds at bay.

Eventually the Captain strode down the gangplank and with a few choice words, that gratefully were taken by the wind, the couple began to board. By this time all the passengers had managed front row seats to watch the spectacle and the woman spying her audience waved and laughed as her husband struggled behind with a few small personal bags.

As soon as they stepped onto the ship the crew sprang into action and ropes were cast, orders shouted and engines beat into life.

"Heavens they don't hang about do they," the woman said and laughed.

"We are late," one of the passengers replied, I thought with more than a hint of sarcasm.

"Really, oh dear," she said oblivious to the nuance. I looked at her companion and he smiled and shrugged his shoulders in a sheepish manner.

"Come on Harold," the woman said and they followed the steward, Bonell. "See you all later," she ended with that laugh and a wave.

The next opportunity we had to engage with this couple was at dinner. Being on a cargo ship dressing for dinner remained a casual affair. None the less the three ladies did their best and the men wore suits. The ship carried twelve passengers to the islands and charged half the price of the regular liners if you could rough it for the twenty days. I had taken the journey many times and enjoyed the freedom of the casual atmosphere. We all stood in the dining room and chatted amicably about our plans, the trip, the weather and then the late comes came in. The middle aged lady rushed up to the two women who were chatting with the steward and myself and butting right in said,

"Hello dearies, what are you drinking?" The women looked a little stunned and I took a step back.

"Er Martinis," one said

"Right, I'll have one too," she said, then introduced herself. "Dolly Lancome and my husband Harold Lancome. Well of course he'd be a Lancome too, silly me." And then she laughed. A throaty, nasal type noise that spluttered into life then hee-hawed for what seemed like several minutes ending in a very undignified snort not dissimilar to a farm yard animal. The women watched the performance fascinated then as the noise died they jumped out of their reverie and introduced themselves and I bowed and said,

"Mr. Weatherness," and held out my hand.

"Oh pleasure," she gripped my hand and pumped vigorously hoping I thought to strike oil.

"Harold, this is Mr. Weatherness. What a treat. Harold held out his hand and Mrs. Lancome passed me over to her husband. He took my hand with a wet fish grip and smiled.

"Nice to meet you," and sort of juggled my hand a bit then slid from my grip making me feel like I should wipe my hand on a napkin or something.

"Yes, likewise," I said and looked around for an excuse to exit. Bonell provided my alibi by sounding the gong for dinner and we all began to sit down at the long table. It didn't take long and the three women were cackling and ordering martinis from the one steward. He was a good natured chap and, as the custom, had been tipped handsomely before the voyage began so knew just how much service to meter out to each passenger.

It is my experience when travelling that where one sits is where one stays. So it can be quite important to eye your companions and use all your skill to judge a good all rounder for company. Many a time I have been stuck with a complete bore or someone whose table manners resemble a pig at the trough. So I ran my experienced eye over my eleven travellers and watched with interest as they began to play musical chairs.

The two women, who we found out later were sisters, stuck together like glue, sitting down next to a Mr. Pritchard who exhibited more than one annoying habit, the least of which was talking with his hands. They fluttered, stabbed, pointed and generally kept themselves entertained throughout his discourse on the merits of beef over fish.

Bonell hovered expectantly so I sat next to Mr McDonald, a trader of spices and a young man called Jack Trimble who, at first glance, seemed sensible and steady. As our meal progressed my dining partners began to relax a little and we exchanged our short histories. Mr McDonald was more interested in his meal than talking and grunted a few replies to our polite questioning and Jack was on his way to visit relatives on one of the many islands, but this was as far as we progressed because sitting diagonal to us was Mrs. Lancome and her laugh. As much as we tried to have a conversation Mrs. Lancome prevented it. Dolly Lancome held court over the entire long table and private digressions were out of the question. Mr. Lancome sat meekly at her side chomping his way through corned beef and vegetables then comport and tinned cream and never uttered a word. His wife made up for his lack of conversation with a diatribe of gossip, of whom we didn't have an idea, anecdotes of which we weren't interested and jokes that were more suited to the bar. It was, we all hoped, only the excitement of the travel that found Dolly in high spirits and not, we feared a portent of things to come.

When Bonell had cleared away we moved to the bar cum lounge and it is here friendships are forged. This evening there was but one group, us against Dolly Lancome, but if the woman could see a shunning she either hid it well or had the hide of a rhinoceros. There were strained looks, quickly engaging conversations and a rush for the next round of drinks as the woman trotted up to the bar and proceeded to lampoon their small selection of spirits.

"Not even a proper brandy for me favourite cocktail," she said to anyone who would listen. We all pretended we were deaf. Mrs Lancome wasn't backward in coming forward and over the remainder of the evening we found they were travelling to Mr Lancome's new posting. He was a public servant. They had invested badly, bought and sold two houses in various locations and really had no choice, but to, as Mrs Lancome put it,

"Flop around and end up in some God forsaken jungle where the natives eat each other."

I could have pointed out that the Island they were travelling to had all the amenities for civilized living including a decent tennis club with a well stocked bar and an ex pat society that was lively and boasted a theatre group, but I left Mrs Lancome to her head hunters and cannibals, the thought much more alluring. After the ten o'clock bell the evening broke up quite quickly and I rather suspected there would be a few select gatherings later that night in small aft quarters accommodation with but one topic of conversation. I retired to my room which I shared with Mr Foreman a cement contractor with a booming voice and a barrel chest to roll the echo around. Bill Foreman was an easy going chap and as he went through his toilet for the evening he carried on a conversation about all the other passengers and I thought he was going to include me in his summations, but when he had cleaned his teeth the chatter stopped and he fell into bed and was asleep within three heartbeats. I usually like to read a little before turning out the light, but this night my mind turned to the Lancome's. She was a strange kettle of fish there was no denying that and I vowed to keep my council on the voyage lest I be drawn into an 'us and them' showdown. They were a strange couple. She wore bright colours and the latest hair style. Shining eyes, sparking jewellery, not real I imagined as they said their tickets were paid for by the Government and the clothes for all their panache were home made. Mrs Lancome kept the small group of passengers entertained with stories, anecdotes and the odd risqué joke. She was, as they say, the life and soul of the party. Mr Lancome was her side kick. A meek individual, with a sallow complexion and not too much hair to hide a sunburnt head. I could well imagine he had hidden his true character long ago and deferred to Dolly in all things. I turned the light out hoping for a better day tomorrow.

The morning brought a small respite. Dolly was a late sleeper. We neglected to see this would be inversely applied and Mrs Lancome was one of life's stayers because the bar never really closed. Bonell had laid out the breakfast smorgasbord and within the first half hour of the 8 am bell all of the passengers bar two were eating. There was a hushed feeling each knowing that if they didn't finish soon they might have to share their quiet, convivial surroundings with Mrs Lancome. Toast was quickly eaten, bacon and eggs gobbled, porridge shovelled and tea and coffee gulped. I have never been a fast eater, my digestive system rebels and so I ate with my usual care and consideration. The dining room emptied until just Mr Foreman and myself remained and then the doors swung open and Mrs Lancome breezed in followed by her husband. She eyed the picked over fare, the two remaining diners and said,

"Well there had better be coffee or I just cannot function." I wondered what Dolly would look like if she could not function. She summoned Bonell with a press of the bell and told Harold to,

"Get them to make a decent coffee," Harold looked to Bonell and smiled that sheepish little smile he had and Bonell disappeared with the empty coffee pot.

"I'm just a miserable wreck without a coffee." Mrs Lancome said. I stood up to leave and Bill followed my lead.

"You're not leaving are you? Heavens it's only 9ish." We shrugged our shoulders like a vaudeville double act and headed for the door. "Harold, make them stay." Dolly commanded then turned as Bonell returned with fresh coffee. "Who is for a fresh pot?" Dolly implored.

I declined saying I had some papers to attend to and Bill said he needed to send a telegram and we left.

"Whew, that was close." Bill said thumbing the doorway we had just scooted through. I nodded and went up on deck for a smoke. The Arc Julius is an old ship with about a dozen layers of paint over every bleeding rust mark. Her foredeck was laden with boxes of freight and it was here I stood taking the sea air and contemplating a day going over my paperwork.

"It's Mr Weatherness isn't it?" I looked around to see one of the sisters.

"Yes," I hesitated. I had been introduced but her name slipped my mind.

"Stella Wright," and she smiled. She pulled a small cigarette case from her jacket pocket and I obliged with a light. We smoked in silence, the allegiance of the weed enough. Presently Miss Wright finished and we stood looking at the sea.

"I must comment on your tact Mr Weatherness. I admire someone who can...shall we say, keep their council."

"It is a habit of a lifetime in the law I'm afraid. A poker face is part of the course." I looked at my watch.

"Are you in a hurry?"

"Work I'm afraid. Paperwork and all that sort of thing." I excused myself as Miss Wright said

"Lunch then?"

"Yes, lunch."

The bell for lunch sounded at 1 o'clock sharp. Food becomes a focal point on a boat with not much else to do and by the time I had climbed the stairs to the dining room I was the last to arrive. Mrs Lancome was holding court at the table relating her morning without adequate facilities.

"And you'd never guess, but they said we would just have to make do, didn't they Harold." And she laughed, hee-hawing until Bonell came in with the soup. While we waited for our main meal Dolly related a rather funny story about Harold and a trip to the butchers and although he was sitting right next to her he remained unmoved by the anecdote. You got the feeling he was just tagging along to make a double for tennis or a partner for bridge. Dolly was giggling almost too much to deliver the punch line, but he just sat. She managed to control herself enough to eventually get it out and I watched Mr Lancome for some spark, but he just sat and picked his fingernails. Not a titter.

"It was hilarious wasn't it Harold?" she asked him.

"Yes hilarious," Mr. Lancome answered, still studying his nails. We tried to remain detached, but it was an amusing story and as our roast beef was served we were laughing at Mr. Lancome's expense. A deplorable situation, but when Dolly put her mind to it she could deliver a joke like a professional stand up comedienne. We finished with brandy trifle and once again Dolly kept us entertained, this time relating a tale involving one of her relatives and a punch bowl at a christening. I caught Miss Wright's eye as the dishes were cleared away and she understood telling her sister she was going out for a smoke. I followed and we met on the deck.

"Mabel, my sister says Dolly really is alright. You just have to take people as they are."

"Well that is certainly true Miss Wright." I dragged heavily on my cigarette.

"Oh call me Stella Mr Weatherness."

"Right Stella," I tried out her name. "And you can call me Trododniak if you like."

"Trododniak. That is quite a moniker."

"Indeed it is. My father's name a matter of fact. Sort of runs in the family."

"Are you going back to the bar Trododniak?"

"Not just now, more work. And you?"

"Oh yes. Mable promised me a game of cards with the Lancomes."

I let her go and enjoyed the balmy afternoon, the calm sea and the relative quiet save the beating of the engines beneath my feet. I strolled back to my cabin to knuckle down to my studies and as I passed the lounge I heard laughing. It seemed Dolly was holding court yet again.

The dinner bell sounded just as I had packed up my papers and so with a quick freshen up I made my way to the bar. When I reached the door and opened it, once again I noticed I was the last to arrive and everyone was laughing, even Mr. McDonald had a hanky out wiping his teary eyes. Stella called me over and try as she might she only managed to relate half the story before collapsing in laughter before the punch line. I waited and on the fifth attempt Mrs Lancome stepped in and the whole audience went up again in peals of laughter. I smiled indulgently at the tale involving Mr Lancome and a trip to the casino, a pair of heels and a hypnotist and made my way to the bar.

"Oh dearie, you had to be there."

"I dare say." I said taking charge of my whiskey and soda.

As we had had our main meal at lunch, dinner was a light affair with a variety of sandwiches and hot finger food. The food I have found on these freighters is as inventive and tasty as any of the more established ships. We all sat and passed various dished around while Mrs Lancome kept us entertained. Later at the bar I managed to talk to Bill about his work before Dolly roped people in for card games and then after one more quick drink I slipped out before the end of an episode about Harold and a Christmas cracker and retired to my cabin. It was well into the night when Bill staggered in and flopped on his bunk. He giggled once or twice and then was out to it. I fleetingly thought about Harold and the ribbing he was receiving and then fell, once again, into sleep.

Every meal we were kept entertained, Dolly having a captive audience.

"It must be just a hoot travelling with Harold?" Stella said one evening after a funny incident involving Harold and a policeman.

"Oh Harold," she said a matter of fact, " Harold doesn't have a sense of humour. None what so ever. You can be splitting your sides about something and Harold the love doesn't see it."

"How does one go through life like that?" Jack asked.

"Oh, I don't know, he gets by don't you dear?" Harold nodded and studied his scotch and water. "I met him and it was love at first sight. Wasn't it dear?" Harold nodded.

"Poor smuck," Mr Foreman said one evening as the Lancome's arrived. I sipped my drink not wanting to add editorial comment and further the conversation. I had travelled too much and too far to not understand human nature just a little. Once one comments sides are taken and cliques emerge and then the whole trip is overshadowed on who sides with whom. Mrs. Lancome gravitated towards the ladies sitting by the window and greeted them with her customary

"You'll never guess," as she sat down for a cracking story you might wonder what could possibly happen on a trading ship that only took twelve passengers.

You would think Harold might retire early and get away from the ribbing his wife enjoyed so much. At first we enjoyed her jokes but soon they became embarrassing as Harold always featured and our laughs were at his expense. He was a good natured man and took it, rarely even raising an eyebrow. I could imagine the rows in their cabin as Mrs Lancome was put in her place. But for her part she seemed oblivious to her victim's feelings.

Mrs Lancome had found her place in the group and none could usurp her reputation for a gay time. Other jokes were bandied about in the dining room and later at the bar as the passengers vied to top the bill, each joke funnier than the last. But Mrs. Lancome always had one more, some even earning the adverb hilarious. There was no denying they were funny anecdotes and one might have laughed long and hard, which some of the passengers and crew did, but when the victim was sitting in the same room, it just didn't seem right.

"I don't know how she does it, night after night." Stella said to me as we enjoyed our cigarettes.

"Quite."

"I mean, there is no denying they are funny. Mabel said she must be making them up, but I'm not convinced. How about you Trododniak?"

"I have not considered the question. Yes they are funny, but I will reserve my judgement on the second proposition."

"Spoken like a true lawyer."

"A Magistrate actually. I am the resident for this area all the way to the tip of Australia."

"Oh."

"Quite." And we left it at that.

As our voyage came to its inevitable end Mrs Lancome's audience became weary. Then one evening we were assembled for our penultimate dinner and Bonell decided to do a fair impersonation of Dolly Lancome's laugh. It was a daring act in the circumstances and one designed to bring the house down. He stood centre stage and hee-hawed, his teeth jutting out, his right hand fluttering and a martini in his left hand and ended with an enormous snort to riotous laughter and applause. It was this cacophony that greeted Dolly and Harold as they walked through the door and suddenly the room went quiet. Thick skin or no Dolly could see who was the butt and she tried to bluff her way by saying,

"Started without me? Now that's not right." And walked to the table and sat down, directing Harold to get her a drink. Harold obliged and I think I detected a slight wry smile on his face as he placed his order with Bonell who was trying to keep from giggling.

Our meal was a wonderful concoction of meatloaf and vegetable stew, Bonell pulling out all the stops and to end he produced ice-cream and tinned peaches. We ate with small talk and nary a titter to be heard. Dolly had gone quiet and the passengers subdued. It is customary to present a tipping jar to the steward on this night and so after the meal we handed around the jar and contributed, each complimenting Bonell on a stirling job. When it came to Harold I noticed he was overly generous and wondered at the largess. The evening was very quiet after the ruckus we had been having over the course of the voyage and so I bade my companions good night and retired.

    I walked to the deck for my customary smoke and stayed quite a while looking at the stars knowing I would be at work within twenty four hours and savouring the last few moments of peace and quiet. When I eventually made my way to my quarters I had to walk past the Lancome's cabin and I could hear laughing, a deep booming laughter that seemed to want to go on and on. And it could only be one person, a person who had waited patiently, probably years, for someone to get their comeuppance.

Plate XII

Flora Rhinehart

It happens quite often in country towns. There is a collective consciousness, a shared memory or a list of manners that are adhered to for whatever reason by the locals. It stems from a proximity with each other's lives, a feeling of belonging and a common history.
The Post Office Hotel Camooweal, like so many in North Queensland, served the people and was the hub of the wheel that extended many many miles into the bush. As as the hub, everything revolved around it. The initial town was gazetted in 1884 to be built on a 4 square mile plot and it looked like it never expanded further. I couldn't see any redeeming features in Camooweal and would be glad to leave it to the few hardy inhabitants, the wedge tailed eagles, dingos and the flies.

I had been forced to break my journey because of a flooded roadway and found the only hotel in the vicinity with rooms. The hotelier greeted me with suspicion as I walked into the dark and cool front bar. As my eyes adjusted to the gloom I saw four men glued to their bar stools. They stopped their drinking and stared. I guessed they didn't come across many travellers and anyone on their patch must be vetted with a good look up and down. I passed muster when the landlord handed me my key and the drinkers went back to their past time.

You drinkin', the proprietor asked.

Yes, I said and ordered a welcoming cold beer. There is nothing like the first gulp of a really cold beer to remind yourself what it means to slake a thirst. In that first draft, the flavour, the coolness, the absolute relief is a prayer answered.

The barman introduced himself, Bert Pedowski, he said, then poured himself a bourbon. It's Polish, he added.

To Flora, he held up his glass and the hardy drinkers responded. They knocked back their drinks and then resumed their sitting.

My guess is that you are wondering who Flora is?

Yes, I said. Mr Pedowski looked over the bar and sized up his clients.

Well...it's not too busy, so I'll tell ya. I looked at the four men in the bar and wondered if there ever was a busy time.

Flora Rhinehart, Pedowski said, wasn't what you would call attractive. The first time I saw her, if I'd had a teaspoon I would have gouged me eyes out. I widened my eyes in exclamation.

It happens in life that once in a while the litter comes up with an ugly one. Flora was that one. The Drovotska family were ten in all and Flora came around number nine. I guess if Mrs Drovotska had had Flora earlier she might have called it quits.

The Drovotskas lived on the edge of town scratchin' a livin' in the dirt. They were poor, but did their best. As the family grew up the children moved away - everyone moves away eventually. Pedowski wiped the bar and looked into the distance. I imagined he knew all the young people by name who had left. Towns often die from lack of loyalty. The grass is always greener, but in Camooweal's case, any grass at all would be a welcome surprise. Pedowski roused himself from his thoughts.

So eventually Flora was the only one left. Not suprisin' really. She wasn't likely to get a husband or anythin'. There were some fellas, young enough in the town at that time, but with Flora no-one was really interested. The family kept goats mainly and tried to coax a few veg out of the ground and Mr Drovotska fixed things. Flora looked after the goats.

Shall I tell ya what she looked like? The barman asked. I could see he was going to tell me anyway, so I nodded.

Flora had the brightest blue eyes you could imagine. There were that kinda blue you often see in the sky on a clear day. A blue that was pale yet deep. Pedowski frowned and ruminated on what to say next. Eyes that could look into your soul. She also had a moustache and a hair lip. And she had a mole thing. Pedowski pointed to his chin.

Right here he said. A whopper. Nature dealt her a cruel blow. He shuddered and poured himself another drink. I wondered where the story was leading, but sat silent.

Well one day it was blowin' up a storm. A westie. A mongrel of a wind. The dust gets in eyes and nothin' can stop it. The wind whips up the dirt and it finds its way into every crevice, every crack and the only relief is to stay indoors. Even then it's touch and go.

The four men in the bar, who I didn't think were listening, all nodded and mumbled.

This particular blow lasted three days I reckon. Three days of dust and dirt.

Bert Pedowski ran his finger around his collar and inspected the result, maybe looking for left over dirt.

So it was a stinker. Not a day for walking, but Flora came into town all wrapped up an' lookin' like an Afgan camel herder or somethin'. One of those headscarves wrapped around her face.

We used to have camel herders around this way, Pedowski said. Long time ago they'd trek through here. Now it's the army. They're buildin' a road. The war an' all that.

So this stinker of a day Rhinehart comes into town and he sees Flora all wrapped up and goes crazy for those eyes. Real blue eyes. I don't know where she got 'em from, but they were blue alright.

I don't mind tellin' ya she looked...Bert hunted for a word. Well she looked pretty damn good. He leaned in closer. You can tell a lot about a person by their eyes. Flora walked into town - a good two hours walk I guess and went to order the stores. Now ya think ya know someone an' all that, but you know that day, with the dust and the wind an' everythin' well Flora had on a pair of men's trousers tied with a bit of twine, a white shirt and a scarf and she was a stunner. She had a trim figure that we'd never seen before, and kinda swung her hips like she'd been doin' it all her life. I guess no-one had ever really looked at her besides that mole, but that day she could have passed for a Hollywood star. She made ya look twice, I'm tellin' ya.

So she's at the store gettin' things and Rhinehart come in. Didn't even recognise her is my guess. Bert yelled to the other drinkers,

What ya reckon Mal? Mal nodded.

Now Rhinehart was a tough bastard. Sort of a quiet, dark horse. A tall bloke with a mat of hair and a permanent snarl. He was always squintin' and snarlin' and looked like an angry dingo most of the time. He was all sinew and muscle. Not a scrap of fat. You don't get fat on this land. He didn't talk much. It's like that sometimes. With on-one to talk to when you live outta town, you forget how to talk. Rhinehart lived way outta town. But he didn't forget how to drink. And he was an ugly drunk.

Bert lent down and showed me the top of his head. It looked like he'd been bald all his life and there was a thumbprint of a crater on his crown. He pointed and said - Rhinehart. The other drinkers looked up and Mal said,

Bloody oath.

Anyway, Rhinehart took a likin' to Flora and gave her a lift back to her place. It was out of his way, right on the other side of town out east, but he took her there all the same. It was almost a done deal, so we heard. Well, the family didn't want to miss the opportunity, did they?

Bert looked at me and added, if you know what I mean? And so they kinda offered ol' Rhinehart somethin' if he'd do the decent thing. Well, that's what we all reckon anyway.

And did he? I asked.

Yep. I dunno what the deal was, but Rhinehart up an' married Flora about a month after meetin' her.

Was it about a month Mal?

Mal put his drink down and thought on the question. We all waited for a minute then he said,

Yep.

And then they went to live on Rhinehart's property.

Bert picked at a scab of leftover food on the bar and continued.

Rhinehart lived away to the west. Strictly speaking he lived in the Territory, 'cause the border is only 7 miles from here, but it's God forsaken country any which way you look at it, so it's all the same. It is a good day's ride on a horse if you have a mind to go there. He wasn't young either and we, in the town, never saw much of him. As I said, he'd come in for supplies and stuff.

The scab released its hold on the bar and Bert flicked it to the floor. We looked at its final resting place and then he went on.

At first we all thought it was a piece of luck for Flora. I mean when you don't have much in the way of natural charms you kinda gotta take what comes. She went out west and we didn't see her for quite a while. Not that we were lookin' or anythin', but in a town like Camooweal, well everyone comes into town - eventually. Rhinehart would still come in once a month or so for supplies, but Flora...

Bert sipped his drink and casually picked up a fly swat. He made a half hearted attempt to keep the flies away and continued with the story.

We never saw her.

You drinkin'? He asked me. I nodded and put my shilling on the bar. With my fresh beer Bert picked up the story.

It was about six months and Flora came in on a horse, for the supplies. She had a black eye. We didn't say anything - it's none of anyone's business how things happen, but you wonder just the same, we all did. We all knew Rhinehart could be a bit of a bastard, kicking dogs, floggin' horses and the like, but as I said, what goes on in a marriage ain't anybody's business. Is it?

Bert asked the question and I wondered if it was rhetorical.

Well, we didn't see her for about... Bert thought on the time then asked,

How long would it have been Jacko? Four months? Jacko frowned then nodded.

About four months she came in one day an' lookin' pretty sorry. That ol' mole thing on her face had been cut off. A nasty jagged scar that looked mean. But it kinda improved the overall effect, if you get my drift.

Jacko held up his glass for a refill and Bet indicated he could help himself. He wasn't too fussed with his customers. Jacko casually walked around to the other side of the bar and gave his three companions a refill, then himself. No money changed hands. Small town economics rely on trust.

Well Flora had a sort of different look, kinda vulnerable. You know, that vulnerable woman look. I nodded knowing that look, as I'd seen it many times in the courtroom as women tried to ameliorate their crime.

I'd say she was gettin' better lookin' if it's possible.

You reckon it was like that Jacko?

Jacko nodded.

Anyhow, it was a hot day and she was sweatin'. One of those hot days when you just don't know where to put yourself. The sun beats down and after a while you just wish you were dead 'cause your sweatin' so much. Well Flora was sweatin' and these big welts began to appear on her back through her shirt. We could see 'em and no-one thought they were an accident. You don't get whip marks bakin' cakes and the like. It could only be Rhinehart. We all saw 'em, but well, unless someone says somethin' you can't go accusin' people.

You just don't know the whole story, do you? We all said if that Rhinehart bastard came into town we'd let him know it ain't right.

The next month she rode in an' there was a burn. It was like that. You'd see somethin' and know it's not right, but still, it's not your business. There was a feelin' in town that Rhinehart would get what for if he showed his ugly face. Gradually Flora came in regular for the 'once a month' list. Rhinehart would turn up whenever he felt the thirst. He got to drinking alone 'cause we all felt he deserved it. And every month there'd be somethin' else on Flora. Torn ear, black eye, gash on the hand, bruises around her neck. You name it we saw it all. But the thing was, she never said anything. Not a word, and well you can't just go off half cocked can you?

Bert was trying to assuage his sins.

And every month Flora seemed to get more an' more bloody attractive. Don't ask me how, it just kinda happened. We all felt real sorry for her. Who wouldn't?

So things are kinda normal, you know, when she stopped comin' in. We didn't see her for ages. Rhinehart came in though, more and more. It was one of those benders he gave me this.

Bert pointed to his head. He knocked Wal right out. Bert pointed to the third drinker. So I told him to sling his hook, hit the road an' don't come back for a bit. There was no doubt Flora would have paid the price for his gettin' chucked out.

I asked for a refill and Bert said,

On the house, as he gave me a cold beer. He swatted a fly which had the misfortune to land on the bar mat and with a quick flick it went to the floor.

So we didn't see 'em for a long time. Don't know what they were survivin' on out there - roo and not much else I guess. It'd been a good six to nine months when Rhinehart appeared one day and he slapped a wad on the bar and said he wasn't leavin' 'till it was gone. I didn't want him drinkin' in the bar, but well, we all gotta make a living', if you know what I mean. So I kinda had to let him stay.

You remember that day Jacko?

Yep, Jacko answered.

Well, he'd been at it for a good three hours, drinkin', swearin', talkin'. Talkin' way too much. Too much about everythin'.

I've heard it all in my time, Bert said. People like talkin' about stuff. It's kinda natural to have a yarn at the bar, but Rhinehart, well Rhinehart let all his secrets slip with the drink. Someone, I think it was two-up, Bert pointed to the fourth drinker, asked Rhinehart about Flora.

You remember Two-up?

Two-up nodded.

Then Rhinehart went crazy. If there was a swear word he used it. I'm tellin' ya, if there was a person who needed to keep quiet it was him He practically boasted he broke her arm. He said he whipped her, he beat her. He told us he cut the mongrel off. We all knew what he meant, 'cause we'd seen the scar on her face. It was all I could do to keep the other blokes from takin' him outside and beatin' him senseless. No-one should beat a dog, let alone a wife. I told him if he didn't shut it then I'd have to bloody sling him. I brought the cosh out.

To prove the point Pedowski reached under the bar and produced a small wooden baseball bat and laid it on the bar. I haven't had to use it often, but I bloody will. Pedowski rolled the cosh on the bar. It looked a formidable weapon.

So I said he needed to shut it and Rhinehart looked at me and I knew, I just knew he'd done somethin' bad. Real bad.

Jacko, Mal, Two-up and Wal stopped drinking and looked over our way.

I didn't ask him outright. You can't just accuse someone of somethin' 'cause ya think it. But somethin' wasn't right. I could feel it. Then he said,

I got rid of the kid.

It was one of those times when ya wish ya had a gun. We all put two and two together.

The bastard. Pedowski almost whispered.

We all kept quiet for a bit, stunned I guess, and then Flora bloody just walked into the front bar. I said she'd have to go to the ladies lounge, but she just stood there. She looked real nice. I'm tellin' ya she was pretty easy on the eye. She had a sundress on with little flowers on it and stuff so I guess we didn't look too hard on what was going to happen.

Well she walked right up to Rhinehart, pulled out a rifle and

BAM!

Bert slammed the cosh down on the the bar and we all jumped. She just put one bullet in his head, right between the eyes.

Pedowski pointed to his forehead.

Right between the bloody eyes. He was sittin' right there. Bert pointed to the bar stool next to mine.

I can tell ya - we were stunned alright. Right there in the front bar and she never blinked. Then she knelt down an' felt in his pockets and pulled out some money and put it on the bar.

Drinks all round, she said and turned and calmly walked out. Bert grabbed his wet rag and began to wipe the bar.

So what happened to Flora? I asked. I hadn't heard of a murder investigation from Camooweal.

Dunno. She walked out that door, he pointed, and no-one has seen her since. She finally got the courage, I guess. Rhinehart probably deserved it. A right bastard. I can't imagine what it must have been like livin' with him. I couldn't repeat the things he said that day.

Drink? Bert asked. We all took a refill,

To Flora,

I raised my glass.

Plate XIII

    Pat

I had been invited to speak at the Winton Country Woman's association and found the only time I had free was in late January. Usually, I try not to travel in the summer months. They are oppressive and uncomfortable, but as I had put off the invitation twice previously, I felt obliged.

The day I arrived by train it was a scorcher. Winton was baking in the heat and had been suffering for ten days with extremely high temperatures. Mrs Mitchell met me at the station. A smartly dressed middle aged woman, she had that country look of no nonsense and plenty of common sense. Her short sleeved cotton dress hung loose in the heat and her hat had a large shady brim and I noticed she wore sensible open sandals. She apologised for the weather.

Not your fault, I said following her to her car parked under a gum tree. The streets were deserted as we made our way to the CWA hall.

We just heard it's 116 degrees, Mrs Mitchell said as she parked the car. It's a record I think. She looked at me suffering and added,

We don't stand on too much ceremony out here Mr Weatherness. Feel free to take off your tie and roll up your sleeves. I immediately felt I liked this woman and followed her direction. We walked into the hall past a quaint picket fence and into the relative cool of the verandah.

Drink? Mrs Mitchell said. I'd normally offer a tea, but I have just had a block of ice delivered and so a cool drink might be the go. Now I knew I liked her. I followed her into the small annex, which served as a kitchen and watched her deft hammering at the block of ice. Large chips broke off and she wrapped these in a tea towel and gave them a good whack on the wooden bench top. Then Mrs Mitchell poured the cordial drink over the ice in large glasses and we made our way to the front verandah and sat down. Mrs Mitchell settled back and began to talk.

Your visit is much anticipated Mr Weatherness. We try to bring a little society to the association and I'm sure you will have an enthusiastic audience. I had often taken up speaking engagements around the outback towns. People like to know the judicial system works for those on the land just as well as those who live in the cities. Rough justice is sometimes the norm out in the wilds, but it is comforting to know that there is something that can be relied upon in a crisis. Mrs Mitchell fanned herself with a small oriental fan,

I know the heat might stop some from making the trip, but I know for a fact one person who will come. Never misses. She looked at the deserted street. Pat will come, she said. We sat in silence listening to the cicadas drum their beat. Mrs Mitchell turned to me. We have a bit of time up our sleeve, so I'd like to tell you about Pat. Is that alright? I was cooling down quite nicely and with a refill of lemonade, Mrs Mitchell began.

Winton is a place where things happen. It might not be as big as Mt Isa or as cosmopolitan as Cairns, but we have had our fair share. There was the beginnings of Qantas, the shearers strike and in 1895 Banjo Paterson wrote Waltzing Matilda. I felt Mrs Mitchell was trying to justify the small town's existence. We have the usual characters about the place. Every town has its characters. Well, we have Pat.

Pat grew up just around the corner from here. Mrs Mitchell pointed down the road. The family were builders and it was natural that Pat go into the business. There are always houses to build as the old ones gradually give up or the white ants get them. So Pat went to work for the family as a bricklayer. He was a gregarious fellow. Always with a smile or a joke and helping hand. We never saw him with a girlfriend, but it's sometimes like that. Young men from the country find it hard to hook up with a mate. Available women are few and far between in the outback. She looked at her wedding ring and gave it a twirl on her finger.

I presumed we were talking about a woman and now I realised Pat was a man.

Bricklaying is a hard business. Most people are done in by the time they reach forty. Bad back. Stiff neck, that sort of thing. My husband is a doctor and so he has firsthand knowledge, Mrs Mitchell said. Well Pat was no different. It was a rather nasty accident with a hopper that finished his career. Mrs Mitchell looked at me. Do you know what a hopper is Mr Weatherness? I nodded.

Well my husband, the doctor, said that was the end of work for Pat. Hard labour was out of the question. Mrs Mitchell looked at the shimmering street. Out here there aren't too many jobs to go around. If you can't put your back into it, well, it's hard to find work.

I had read a report recently about the decline of opportunities for those in the outback and readily accepted Mrs Mitchell's facts.

So what happened? I asked.

Well, you'd never think it, but Pat said he was going to write a book. No-one had an inkling that he had it in him, and you'd think that in a small town like Winton someone might have seen that creative streak. We have a small book club here, and a little library, but no authors. Pat said he had a bit of money saved and said that was the plan. Well, there were some in the town thought it just a flight of fancy. Others thought it plain ridiculous. I kept my judgements to myself. Mrs Mitchell fanned herself vigorously and I felt she had to make a point of being seen to be unbiased and not a gossip monger.

But, Mr Weatherness this is not the story. I sipped my lemonade and sat back in the cane chair deep in the shade of the verandah.

No?

No. Mrs Mitchell repeated. You see, Pat had more than a yearning to write a book. More than a desire to pen a masterpiece. Pat wanted a complete change. Pat wanted to be a woman.

Oh. I said.

Oh indeed, Mr Weatherness. Nothing like this had happened to Winton. You can imagine the talk that went through the town. Pat came to Doctor Mitchell and asked him about it all.

I looked at Mrs Mitchell, knowing the confidences of a doctor or lawyers are sacrosanct. Mrs Mitchell saw my query written on my face.

Oh, Mr Mitchell and I keep every confidence. It wasn't me who spread the word. Mrs Mitchell said emphatically. Never-the-less the word soon got out. In a small town your business is everybody's business, she shrugged her shoulders. You may wish to bury a secret out here, but it will turn to dust eventually and blow into every crevice, every house, every crease on the back of your neck. That is the bush, Mrs Mitchell pronounced.

It started with a scarf. Pat went to the draper and bought a silk scarf and tied it around his head. Then there was a white tailored blouse and then a pair of slacks. Sort of the Katherine Hepburn look. We have a draper which caters for the women and you can get

Yvonne Anderson to make up your dresses from the paper patterns. So Pat did just that.

Yvonne said it wasn't easy. Vogue and McCall patterns are made for the female form. But she did her best. Pat's figure was 6ft and barrel chested with wide shoulders and virtually no hips. Yvonne does lovely work. Mrs Mitchell smoothed her dress over her knees and I assumed her outfit was from the local woman. Actually, the women of the town took a motherly interest in Pat; it was the men who were so cruel. Pat couldn't walk down the street and would get more than a snide remark. His friends, people he had grown up with, people he had drunk with in the hotel, now turned on him. His workmates were particularly awful. It was such a shock to see the vitriol from the men. Men who had been part of the fabric of the town. It wasn't what Winton was like. Pat polarized the town. Those that were with the transformation and those that were against.

I was on the affirmative, Mrs Mitchell said. Dr Mitchell and I like to think we are broadminded enough to let people choose their own way in life. But the others. The others in the town thought it was a travesty. An abomination; and so they had a meeting.

And Pat? I asked.

Pat kept quiet. She had her book to write. I noticed Mrs Mitchell had switched the pronoun to she and though this must have been the turning point in the story.

So the meeting was held in the hall and there was quite a turnout. Both sides of the argument were there and if the police hadn't been in attendance there might have been a brawl. It was the liveliest gathering Winton had seen for a while. Ned Whitley brought a gun and said he'd run Pat out of town at the end of his shotgun. Even the Minister said Pat should go and he calls himself a Christian. They used nasty words like decency, normal, and unchristian. The consensus, I'm afraid, was that Winton didn't need people like Pat and they asked Dr Mitchell, as the town physician, to tell Pat she had to go.

I went along for support, Mrs Mitchell said. Pat had lived here all her life. Her family were here. Her relatives were buried here and now the town had turned on her. It was a crime, but we, her friends said, for her own safety, it was better she go. I don't think anyone had been run out of town before. The lynching mob had got their way.

I for one, felt ashamed. We offered to drive Pat to Mt Isa, but she said she would catch the bus. There was a crowd when the bus arrived and they actually cheered as she was boarding. It wasn't a pretty sight. I have never come across bigotry before Mr Weatherness and I didn't like it when I saw it. Pat had on a nice two piece made with a summery cotton and a straw hat. We watched as she made her way down the bus not knowing if she would ever come back. This wasn't the Winton I knew.

Mrs Mitchell looked at the stark white sky from the cool of the verandah. I knew small town politics can be a heady brew. Many a time I had seen the emotions of country folk at boiling point over a perceived crime.

Well, Pat stayed away for about nine months. Those that were her friends tended her house, looked after the garden and such. It was the least we could do. No-one knew if she would ever come back or why she would want to, under the circumstances. We didn't get a letter or postcard. No-one knew where she had ended up. We hoped she was happy where ever it might be.

But she did come back? I said.

Mrs Mitchell nodded,

Mmm. She did. We, at the CWA, have a meeting once a month and it was our August meeting. I was putting out the chairs and in walks Pat.

A surprise I imagine? I questioned.

Quite a surprise. Because not only had Pat returned, she looked different. More feminine. She said Sydney was a world away from Winton in every respect. We all knew what she meant. She had met people who had helped her adjust. There was a broad acceptance of something a bit different. A bit exotic.

Have you been to Sydney Mr Weatherness? Mrs Mitchell asked.

Yes, I said. I went to university there many years ago. It is a vibrant city.

I haven't been myself, Mrs Mitchell said, but Pat said, if there is one place a person should go before they die, it must be Sydney.

Well, Pat fell into the right crowd of people, Mrs Mitchell stressed *right* and I made an educated guess on the nuance, and it was then that her transformation really took place. A whole new wardrobe, hair, nails and all that sort of thing. Acceptance of who you really are is a great morale booster. Pat didn't have to hide or pretend in Sydney.

Mrs Mitchell leaned forward and stopped fanning herself. Apparently, she began; there is a lively crowd with the same inclinations in the city. Pat fell in with likeminded people.

But, Mrs Mitchell stressed, this country, she spread her arms wide, has a pull on you if you are brought up on the land. Winton was home and Pat missed it. When you come from the dust and the flies and the heat it is in your bones. No matter where you end up there will always be a little red dust under your skin. I think it is the wide open spaces, the endless horizon and the night sky. You just can't get that in the big smoke. She resumed her fanning.

I nodded. There is nothing like the night sky out in the middle of nowhere. Stars so bright they look like you could reach them with an outstretched hand. Smeared brush strokes of light and patterns that test your imagination and make you think of God.

Pat wanted to come home, Mrs Mitchell said. The city had given her the self confidence and a new wardrobe. The CWA meeting that month was quite lively as we quizzed Pat on the latest fashions, hats, gloves and gossip. Pat had fallen in with some Americans and they opened her eyes. This wasn't Hollywood at the cinema, these were real people who have a fashion sense the Australians could never hope to achieve. She had seen it all and we just gobbled up every morsel of her Sydney experience. It's not often you get to hear it from the horse's mouth, so to speak. Yvonne was quite busy after that with copying new dresses from the city, courtesy of Pat. We didn't know how the rest of the town would take to the news, but Pat had another surprise up her couture sleeve.

She had written a book. And what's more it was quite a good book, about her life.

Quite an accomplishment, I said knowing to write well is hard work.

Pat had brought a box of book from her publisher in Sydney and put them in the library and in the window of the drapers. She was even in the paper and on the radio such was her fame. And then all of a sudden people who had cheered as she boarded the bus, now thought she was an asset to the town. A celebrity.

Can you believe it?

I can, I said.

Mrs Mitchell looked at her watch. She should be along any minute. As if on cue a Studebaker Roadster drove up and stopped under a large gum tree. I watched as a tall, elegantly dressed woman stepped out, adjusted her handbag and waved.

Mrs Mitchell waved back and we waited for the woman to reach the shade. I stood up.

Mr Weatherness, this is Pat. I held out my hand.

Plate XIV

Albert Barrett & Friend.

There are some hours of the day that are no good for anything. Not enough time to start something new, too much to allocate to a cup of tea.

I found myself with time on my hands and decided to visit Miss Ricks Reads; the local book exchange. It was a small establishment tucked neatly between a barber's pole and the only green grocer in the small town of Charters Towers. I expected the usual suspects and indeed there was romance aplenty and stacks of well thumbed short thrillers. I strolled along the shelves looking for something -not sure if I'd find anything that took my fancy and might entertain me for a day or two when I spied a small volume bound in purple cloth with elegant gold lettering.

A. Barrett & Friend held no more than 100 pages and for its discount price seemed a bargain. It was only when I proffered my purchase to the woman behind the counter, and the following story she told me that I realised I could have saved my money and just asked her about A. Barrett.

Albert Barrett, she began, was a local man. He was of the other persuasion. Those that keep their private passions very private. He possessed a young face, full of youth. Quite pretty actually. Albert went about his daily life and people in the town took no notice.

Miss Ricks indicated a spare chair and I sat down to listen.

Albert Barrett was a kindly lad. He didn't excel in anything in particular, but then he never fell behind. His was a life of order, as his parents had had him much later in their life than is usual. And as is with all latecomers to the family, he was born into a set routine, a certain way of doing things. He didn't have it in him to rebel in his teenage years, like other young folk around the town and school just slipped by without a murmur of discontent. In fact in the school graduation photograph his was the face that people recognised, but could never quite put a name to, and so it was that Albert entered his adult life in obscurity. Now most young men look to catch a girl about this time in their development, but Albert never went looking. He obtained a job in accounting and watched the world go by at a distance. Things carried on much the same for about 6 years or so and then...

Miss Ricks paused for effect,
And then Mr William Snubbs came to town.

A more flamboyant creature you couldn't find. He dressed outrageously in cerise and aqua. His shirts were from the better end of the city, his trousers all the way from England. And his shoes. His shoes were from Italy, handmade.

Miss Ricks sat back satisfied she had painted a vivid picture.

William Snubbs lavished his friends, of which there were many, with presents and was what a small country town would call a colourful character. The locals had never seen anyone like Mr Snubbs and there was great speculation as to where he came from, what he did for money and what he would do next.

Miss Ricks paused and asked if I'd enjoy a cup of tea. With the kettle on, she continued.

Well what Mr Snubbs did next was to captivate Mr Barrett. Albert didn't see it coming and Mr Snubbs bowled him over for 6. We all, in the town, thought dear Albert might swing on the other side of the fence and Mr Snubbs confirmed it. It was a classic romance you might say. Albert, at first, was flattered. Here was this gorgeous man, dressed in the finest silk ties, waistcoats and dark exquisitely cut suits. A man who could order caviar and oysters like ham and eggs. A man who knew and cited as his friends famous writers, Prime Ministers and artists courting an accountant, our local boy called, Albert Barrett.

Albert rebuffed him. It was one thing to fantasise and quite another to declare yourself in your home town. The refusal was polite, but to William it was a challenge. There were flowers. There were presents and cards and invitations to dinner, luncheon, picnics and swims. All this made Albert weaken. He tried to resist, albeit in a faint hearted way and then he said yes to an invitation for birthday party. William's birthday bash was to be a grand occasion. The town was in a frenzy at the preparations. Packages arrived at the post office with tins of food with strange sounding names. Musicians turned up and took over the hotel. It was an exciting time. We, as a town, felt proud that our Albert was going to be there. He bought a suit from the draper, made himself as dapper as possible then presented himself at the hotel. What went on in the pub was the topic of discussion for weeks afterwards, but the outcome was obvious. Albert moved out of home and into the suite of rooms at Tolano's Excelsior Hotel.

Miss Ricks explained, Albert used to live at home with his ailing parents and devoted his time to their care and comforts, but when William prised him away the old Barretts were forgotten.

Just like that! She snapped her fingers.

Mr Snubbs took care of Albert's every need; so much so that Albert quit Stacey, Rider & Brown Accountants and committed his time to William.

There were parties. There were charabancs and holidays, but they always returned to the Excelsior Hotel. We couldn't get over the change in Albert. He dressed with style. He knew the difference between Russian and other caviar and he drank copious amounts of champagne. It was, it seemed to the town, a coming out. There were some around town who thought it scandalous, the way the two carried on. Some thought it brought a bit of life to the main street and only a few who thought it none of their business.

Miss Ricks brought out a packet of plain biscuits and refreshed the tea pot.

Life to Albert and William was one big excursion and it looked like they would just go on having fun until they died. Where the money came from no-one was sure, but it was an endless supply. Bohemia came to town and we saw all sorts traipse through. Arty types, actors, writers and any number of poets. Men with women, often two, women with men and other women. All made their way to Snubbs rooms at the Excelsior.

I looked at the bookish woman. She seemed quite proud of her small association concerning the parade of life's artistic clique.

Then one day, for no apparent reason William Snubbs came over all queer and Doctor Calloway was called. Doctor Calloway has been with the town as long as it's been a town and nothing was new to him. It didn't take long for the news to spread around that Snubbs had had a turn, and it was his heart. Well, there were flowers, presents and cards. Joy, at the post office, was run off her feet with the flood. Of course Albert took care of everything. The Doctor said he needed rest. Complete rest. And so he did. But then...

Miss Ricks pulled at my coat sleeve with her old bony fingers and leaned in close.

William Snubbs decided to write his memoirs.

Miss Ricks sat back after delivering the salient point. I was yet to find out how important this piece of information was to the story.

Stationary was ordered from the city. The finest books, pens, paper and portfolios of writing materials. Supplies laid in for the duration with French champagne, brandy and Italian pastries and as Albert was a proficient typist he was charged with taking the role of secretary. William's writerly friends came to give him support and encouragement and the town imagined many a night was spent up in those rooms drinking expensive champagne talking about books.

There was, throughout the town, much talk regarding the book The locals felt William would be sure to give them a mention in the best seller, after all they reasoned, he had made their little hamlet home for many years as well as taking a local lad under his wing. It was through Doctor Calloway that the townsfolk received updates. Mr Snubbs was collecting material about his time in Italy. Mr Snubbs was making notes on the birthday party extravaganza. Mr Snubbs was well into his first draft. Soon people were boasting that they had 2 pages in chapter 3, 6 lines in the picnic episode or a paragraph devoted to the time they helped William in some small way. It became quite a talking point - everyone was at it, everyone that is except Albert Barrett. Albert kept silent.

He would not be drawn on the book. When William eventually convalesced enough to take a short stroll down the main street, people would ask -how's the book progressing Mr Snubbs? It as a familiar topic of enquiry and as Albert stood silent and protective of his charge no-one thought to enquire as to Mr Barrett's trammelled life. It was all about William Snubbs.

Miss Ricks sat back and took the last of the plain biscuits and said,
And I suppose it might have been so, except for Albert's inner demons.
I hesitated to ask, but it seemed Miss Ricks was waiting for me to say something.
Inner demons?
She took the cue.
Albert it seemed was not in the book. If the manuscript was to be read, William didn't have a soul mate, a partner, a companion. He travelled life's road as a bon vivant looking for friends where he found them. Mr. Snubbs omission of Albert was a lie. It was, Miss Ricks explained, a mighty big sticking point in Mr Barrett's craw. The manuscript was typed in dribs and drabs and as Mr Snubs recovered his health the writing was forgotten, or so it seemed.
Life returned to something like normal when William Snubbs fell ill once again. Another relapse, we all thought, but this was something else. He was seriously ill. Doctor Calloway was called, but he was at a loss. There was talk of another heart turn, but the Doctor didn't confirm it. Mr Snubbs took to his bed and Albert, who had cared for his elderly parents all those years ago, took on the role of nurse maid once again. His devotion was legendary. There was nothing the man wouldn't do for his friend, but try as he might William sank ever lower into ill health. It seemed that there was nothing anyone could do, and eventually, at the very

end, William's friends were called and he said his goodbyes. It was a sobering time in the town as those near and dear to William Snubbs came to pay their last respects. People poured in from all over, and our little town had quite the cosmopolitan feel about it. William Snubbs had touched so many lives in so many ways.

Albert arranged a beautiful funeral. All the town came out in force for the event. William Snubbs had a grand send off in the tradition of his life. It was quite an occasion.

Miss Ricks closed her eyes and a smile played over her lips as she must have remembered the day.

So what of Albert? I held up the book. The spindly woman opened her eyes and licked her lips.

Albert fell into lethargy. He sloped along the street. He shuffled to the shops and generally mourned and moped. And he didn't look well himself. His face took on a grey pallor and his eyes had a sunken haunted look about them. We all knew, or thought we knew the reason, Miss Ricks said. He had a lot of things to organise and as the Doctor was concerned for Albert he offered to help with the more practical side of things. It was just on the off chance that Doctor Calloway picked up a box of odds and ends to help one afternoon that he saw to his surprise a bottle of pills. Pills he didn't prescribe. He questioned Albert about the vial and Albert denied all knowledge of the medicine, but Doctor Calloway didn't come down in the last shower and he wasn't convinced so easily. He took the pills away and...

Here Miss Ricks shuffled her thin frame in close,
And?"

And they were poison. Miss Ricks repeated the word. Poison. She raised her eyebrows in exclamation.

So...? I began, when Miss Ricks held up her hand and followed my one syllable with a stern school teacher look. I shut my mouth and waited.

Of course the Doctor was more than a little suspicious. Here was a bottle of poison with no name on it, and a man had just died. If it wasn't for Albert's inconsolable grief one could very well think the worst of Albert Barrett. As it was he became maudlin, morose and quite the recluse

Eventually life returned to normal in our little outback town and as Albert was rarely seen, he was forgotten. And so it would have continued, but for Joy Leichhardt from the post office. Miss Leichhardt gets holidays once a year and always goes to her sister's house in the big smoke. So Miss Leichhardt went for her customary two weeks and when she returned she brought back from a book shop, a slim volume bound in purple with gold lettering.

Miss Ricks smiled. I nodded and looked at my purchase.

It didn't take long for the town to get the story.

Mr Barrett had taken Mr Snubbs work and somehow made it his own and in the process maligned William Snubbs. Instead of the bon vivant, the philanthropic party goers, Mr Snubbs was portrayed as mean, demanding and a ruin of a decent man. And Albert, well Albert was the victim. He cared for his friend with a devotion that called for the word saint. It was not the relationship the town had seen. If the book was to believed, Mr Snubbs had used Mr Barrett and sucked him dry.

The story contained a gritty jealousy, a fat spat of envy and a blister of hatred. If it was to be believed, William resented Albert more than one man is able and still live a decent life. Mr Snubbs was portrayed as conniving and secretive and took great pains to stick it in the eye of his devoted partner.

But it was the ending that struck the town with terror.

I flicked to the back page when Miss Ricks put her claw on the book and closed it.

Albert, after a rather vivid fight, could take it no longer and made plans to commit a murder. But as fate would have it the pill was never delivered by the trusting hand and William died of heart failure.

So he didn't poison him?

Well...Miss Ricks casually picked at her nails. We all thought that too. The book was a fanciful fictional tale that was close to the bone, but no one in the town believed in murder. But then the book became a success. Sales increased to the extent that Albert came out of hibernation and was giving interviews, talks and signings. But he had changed. Something had happened to Albert. He became skitty, looking over his shoulder, furtive and had a wild look in his eyes. A look that only the guilty have.

And there was something else. Just a hint of maliciousness.

There was quite a buzz around the town regarding the book. Sales did well - very well for of course townsfolk were looking for a mention in the book.

Miss Ricks smiled at me. I have a small section in chapter three. I nodded and smiled back as her hands fluttered about in the air.

Then, at the end there was a small few paragraphs. They were written in a matter of fact hand. In those lines there was the hint of intent.

I flicked to the back and read.

A lie can poison the body as well as the soul.

I shot a look at Miss Ricks. She countered it with one word,

Poison.

That phrase was all the people needed to know. William Snubbs was poisoned. Albert Barrett administered the pill and that was that. Of course there are two sides to every story and the town took sides. Some said Albert couldn't have done it. Others were convinced he was guilty. All through the furore Mr Barrett kept silent and the book sales soared.

Miss Ricks looked me in the eye. There is some notoriety in being notorious.

The less he said the more his story grew. But Albert was riddled with guilt. Guilt about the book and...

So did he? I asked.

They found a small note. Albert Barrett died of his own hand. The question of Mr Snubbs demise hung in the air.

Doctor Calloway confirmed Mr Snubbs died of an excess of living. Nothing more. But it was Mr Barrett's confession to hasten the journey that was chronicled in the note. He was sick of playing second fiddle to the more outgoing William. The last straw came at his omission from the book. The slight was too much to bare. He had procured some poison and was slowly killing William, one drink at a time.

And so...Miss Ricks looked across the table at me,

Albert Barrett died of a guilty conscience? I offered. This small mousey woman who had held me captive with her story sat back and looked like the cat who'd got the cream. I raised my eyebrow in enquiry.

Albert died of accumulative poison. She sat back satisfied, and then could not contain her smugness at knowing the truth.

It seems, according to Dr Calloway, that Albert had also been ingesting poison for some time. The Doctor had traced the pills to William Snubbs. The same poison was found in poor Albert's blood. William Snubbs was heartily sick of Albert's attentions and had been planning his demise. Albert's attempt at suicide was just the one tablet, but it was enough to break the camel's back.

Miss Ricks started to gather our afternoon tea things and I looked at my small purchase and wondered if I needed to read it at all.

She cleared away, then asked, anything else? I shook my head and paid the bargain price. It was later, as I checked out of the Excelsior Hotel, that I realised I'd left the small purple bound volume with gold lettering on the bedside table - and there it stayed.

Plate XV

Lola & Reverend Stanley Pinks

Cooktown is a frontier town. Always was and always will be. It is the first stop after the wilderness of the Top End and attracts life's misfits. Those that don't quite fit the mould of suburban life. It also attracts people who see it as their one last chance. A chance to redeem themselves, find themselves or absolve themselves. People come to Cooktown to run away.

The steamer dropped me off on my way to the Torres Straits as I had three duties to perform. While I waited for my transport to take me to lodgings, which up here could take 10 minutes or half a day, such is the lackadaisical nature of the place, I took a walk up a small hill and found myself in front of the puritanical goodness of the Methodist Church and I briefly wondered at the size of the congregation, given Cooktown's itinerant nature.

A man in shirt and shorts saw me and waved. I waved back and he began to walk over. Once he reached the path he held out his hand and I took it in a gesture of friendship.

David, he introduced himself.

Trododniak Weatherness, I replied, adding - a family tradition I'm afraid to his quizzical look.

I'm the caretaker, he hoiked his thumb towards the church.

You do a good job, I indicated the tidy grounds. David smiled and lent on his hoe,

Used to be just a patch of dirt once, he paused - when Reverend Pinks was with us.

Moved on? I asked, knowing the church regularly move their ministers around for whatever reason. David shook his head,

Died. He pointed to a small well groomed cemetery further up the hill. Buried there. I'll show you if you like?

We walked the few hundred paces up the hill to a plot of land containing head stones, obelisks and Chinese shrines.

Over here, David led me through the aisles until we were standing in front of a large wrought iron fenced plot with one headstone.

A family plot? I inquired.

Shall I tell you about Reverend Pinks? I nodded and followed David to a wooden bench under a mango tree and we made ourselves comfortable. He put his hoe down, took out a cigarette and I took his lead, lighting up one of my own.

Reverend Pinks was an idealist. He had an innate belief in his fellow man. His goodness - his worth. I had seen too much in my tenure as a magistrate to believe in altruistic motives. I have found on the whole, men do thing for selfish reasons. What's in it for me is the catchphrase of modern man. David blew out some smoke.

He came to Cooktown in 1932 from Dubbo Victoria and saw it as an opportunity. He also brought his young wife. Lola Pinks was the perfect minister's wife. Petite, demure, perky and devoted. Stanley Pinks was a lucky man indeed. The Pinks breezed into town like someone who'd never been further north than Goondiwindi and threw himself into the task. This was Stanley's first real parish. He had been attached to a church in Dubbo, but this was his first posting where he had control. Not that there was much to control. The congregation consisted of two families, a caretaker, David pointed to himself, and a spinster organist. Cooktown is a long way from Dubbo Mr Weatherness. I agreed.

Do you know the sort of people that come to Cooktown? It was a rhetorical question. People running away from their wives or the police. I smirked at the apt description. The last thing on their minds is redemption. So Reverend Stanley though he could change all that. He though if he just wooed the customers they would come, except there are no free offers in the Methodist church. But the Pinks were young and enthusiastic and that must count for something.

Yes, I guess it does, I said.

So the Pinks began a programme of helping the needy. There were clothes drives, food drives and it worked for a bit. People around here like to get something for nothing. Who doesn't? David looked at me and I agreed. So that was when Mrs Pinks, Lola, came up with the idea of a free lunch.

Ah, the free lunch, I said. David nodded.

At first nothing could dampen their spirits. It was frontier territory and they just had to try harder. It was a challenge they said. How could they lose - God was on their side. Stanley was a willowy fellow - all arms and legs and a permanent smile. He'd walk around like the sun was shining just for him, with Mrs Pinks in tow. He'd visit every family giving them tickets to 'The Greatest Show on Earth'. That was his catchphrase you see. The Greatest show on Earth, not meaning him of course, but God. David stopped talking and pondered the words. So he eventually gathered one or two, but the church mainly was empty. This went on for about the 5 months, I reckon. David said crossing his ankles and leaning back on the bench. It was a dismal beginning really. After all his high hopes. After all his grand ideas the congregation was no bigger 'cause two of the originals had died. Officiating at their funerals was the only occasion Reverend Pinks could actually shine. People went on with their lives and the Methodists didn't figure at all. Reverend Pinks was a mighty speaker though. David smiled at the thought. His sermons were grand things. There was something about the way he threw himself into the talk that made you admire the man. It was one of the highlights of my week, listening to those sermons. He had a way of getting to the the nub, or the moral of the story and he could grip you with his voice and have you on the edge of your seat. I've never encountered such a powerful speaker, not before, not since.

He'd stand there at the pulpit and you felt he was talking to just you. Mrs Pinks would sit in the front seat and her eyes would be glued to her husband for the whole 45 minutes. David went quiet and I guessed he was reliving the moments. He roused himself,

But I was telling you about the free lunches, he said.

Yes, I replied.

Well, Mrs Pinks had the idea that if we could tempt people to come for lunch, while they were eating Reverent Stanley might talk and once they heard the word of God, then they were sure to come again. It was a good idea, and a free lunch did tempt people at the beginning, but the obligation of sitting through a sermon was too much - even with roast meat and veg. Mrs Pinks would labour away in the kitchen over at the manse. But the Reverend didn't want o upset his wife, she'd worked hard and so he thought on a plan. He would eat two or three lunches and she would never know. He didn't want to disappoint his wife after all the effort she put in. She was a mighty good cook. Roast beef, potatoes, carrots and then pudding. I was sworn to secrecy about the arrangement. I even polished off two lunches for a good month before my wife said enough is enough. We gained one or two for a Sunday. I think they thought they would get another feed. Well Mrs

Pinks kept cooking and Mr Pinks kept eating and as all things in life there are consequences to ones actions. It wasn't long before Reverend Pinks needed to let out his trousers Nothing too drastic in that for a bloke. It happens to us all at some point. David looked at his own waist and sucked in his gut, then let it loose again.

Meanwhile Mrs Pinks had been working hard and, always petite, she became thin. She had the idea to offer Sunday lunch too. If they couldn't share what little they had what sort of Methodists were they, she said to my wife, Beth.

Lola started a garden to grow the potatoes and onions. She was very inventive with her meals, eking out the meagre meat allowance. And the reverend kept eating.

It was about a month before their first wet season when the secret finally came out. Reverend Pinks had ballooned out and nothing fitted anymore. He had been eating for three people and it showed. We all thought there would be a hullabaloo, but Mrs Pinks said she was flattered that her husband thought so much of her. And so she began to cook just for him. Tarts, trifles, biscuits and buns. Lola made friends with the Chinese and they could get anything in the way of ingredients. She lavished her culinary attentions on the Reverend. Nothing was too much trouble, no dish too extravagant. Reverend Pinks had found his appetite. It was amazing how Mrs Pinks made the money stretch. Then, as the Reverend expanded, so did his congregation.

He was becoming 'the Greatest show on Earth'. People would come to see the fat man. You can't imagine how big he was. He was in the local paper, a celebrity. David blew out his cheeks and held his arms wide. The local aborigines lined up at the door just to get a look. The Chinese came to gawk. No-one had seen such a sight. They dubbed him Porky Pinks. There is a picture somewhere of three small children holding hands around his girth. Of course, he knew his size was making him an attraction, but Stanley thought it might be his gift from God. All the hullabaloo was flattering too. People came from everywhere to look and as a grand speaker Reverend Pinks was a natural with the good natured crowd.

God works in mysterious ways, he often said. The Reverend said he was an instrument, and he certainly played it for all it was worth. Mrs Pinks on the other end of the scale was thin.

The church had a decent size congregation just to watch the Reverend in action. And Stanley rose to the occasion. He was a commanding presence. He would rouse the congregation with his sermons. You could see it in their faces. Once under his spell, he could make you believe in anything. His size just reinforced that anything was possible with the will of God. They had to reinforce the dais in the church and he had a special chair made to accommodate his size.

David looked at me. Can you see, Mr Weatherness, a man who was as wide as he was tall? We sat still thinking on the dimensions and I asked,

What of his health? David lit another smoke.

He wasn't spritely anymore. He huffed and puffed about the place, but on the whole he was happy. And Mrs Pinks cooking was too good to pass up. He loved her you see, so it was natural he just put away what was in front of him.

And Mrs Pinks? I asked.

A labour of love. David drew heavily on his cigarette then flicked the butt to the ground.

Or so we thought, he added.

It was one of those days when you can feel a cyclone brewing. When the air gets sucked out of town and you're left with the heat. The birds go to ground and it's like the whole place is just waiting, waiting for something to happen. People can go a bit crazy on a day like that. Tempers fray and the slightest thing can set a person off.

I nodded knowing that feeling of expectation before the wind.

It was hot. I mean really hot. The heat from the sun is so fiery that it burns your skin and you'd like to kill yourself to out of the heat, only you can't be bothered for even that. I don't know why people live here. It's so hot. You sweat just sitting still.

The reverend was sweating. Dripping, but we all were that day. Even with all his extra weight, when I arrived, I could tell something wasn't right. He said he'd been up half the night with indigestion and the other half arguing with his wife.

I asked him if he was alright, and he said it was something he ate. Never a truer word has been said when he just fell down - dead.

Heart attack? I asked.

So they say. He hit the floor with an almighty thud, broke two floor planks and a joist, and Mrs Pinks came running. She just stood there for about a minute, in shock I thought, then went back inside wiping her hands on her apron. I was at a loss on what to do. I called the doctor and he looked the Reverend over and said we needed to get him out of the sun.

The tropics can be a powerful motivator when you have a dead body on your hands. Stanley needed special consideration. We called in an army engineer because of the problem. It took a whole day to work out the logistics while the ice factory worked overtime. It was decided to cut the floor and lower Stanley to a waiting truck parked under the house. And while all this was happening the crowds began to grow.

There has to be some dignity in death, David said as he shuffled the ground with his bare foot. The Reverend had none. His removal to the church was like a side show. And all the while Mrs Pinks said nothing.

Getting him indoors and on ice took the best part of two days, in the heat. We had a sort of ramp with roller wheels and a block and tackle hooked up to the vestry wall. Tom, a ringer, said he moved dead horses like that, so that's what we did. Still, it wasn't easy. Then we had to get ol' George to make a coffin. A big one. In the end he built it around Stanley and reinforced the bottom with a solid slab of teak from an old ship at the slipway. Time was ticking in the heat.

His funeral was the biggest congregation the church had seen. You don't see a box that big ever day. People packed the place to get a look. It was in the papers, such was the crowd. A minister came from down south to officiate, but I think he was more interested in the notoriety than a decent send off for Stanley. I guess Stanley finally got people to see the greatest show on earth.

I thought that was the end of the story and looked over to the grave. David put his hand on my arm for me to remain seated.

Well it wasn't one day after we finally put Stanley in the ground, David pointed to the grave site, and Mrs Pinks threw out the stove. Small as she was, she humped that cooker to the back door and pushed. It lay in the yard on its side. Then we heard she had been seen at Li Ng's house, more than once. He was the grocer. It didn't take long for the rumours to spread.

I look after the grave. If you don't repack the soil when he starts to go... not to be disrespectful or anything, but, well you can't have that amount of meat in the ground and not get a bit of subsidence. Mrs Pinks hasn't been near the place.

We looked at the large plot, neatly tended and I revised my thoughts on it being a family plot. Obviously the whole thing was taken up by the reverend.

Lola left town with Ng about a month after, and that was the last we saw of her.

So was the Reverend's death suspicious? I asked.

She killed him with his knife and fork, then threw the murderous intend into the back yard.

We looked at the headstone on Reverend Pinks grave.

The Greatest Show On Earth.

People still come to look at the grave you know. He was quite a man. Larger than life.

And Lola?

Someone saw her in Melbourne, running a Chinese restaurant of all things. Said she would never go back to the tropics. Hated the heat, the mosquitoes, the wet. David frowned.

Cooktown is like that. Nothing is what it seems.

Pearling fleet TH Isl.

Plate XVI

Hal & Gloria Wafflebach

The Torres Straits are a far flung string of islands closer to New Guinea than Australia, but belong to Australia they do and are often the first or last port of call to somewhere else.
I had had a full week on Thursday Island as one of the first load of civilians to be allowed back after the evacuation in 1942, and decided to take a boat to Badu Island and stay the weekend in seclusion and relaxation. Badu had a reputation for head hunters in its past, but missionaries and pearls tamed the population. Island life in the tropics is slow, lazy and relaxing if you have nothing to do. If you are trying to run a business it can be the bane of your existence. Luckily I had nothing to do, and so I took a good book and found a seat under a shady tree with a cool breeze and began to unwind.

Why it is, I will never know, but the minute you begin to read someone wants to talk. I had just settled in when a man walked over to me and stated the obvious.

Reading I see.

Yes, I said looking up. The gentleman had on cowboy boots and blue jeans, a checked open neck casual shirt and a hat, which I thought might be a Stetson.

Howdy, he offered his hand. Hal Wafflebach. He pronounced his name in an unmistakeable American accent, the soft German bach turning into a broad sounding back. I put my book down and shook his hand.

Trododniak Weatherness, I offered. He looked askew and I gave my usual explanation.

A family tradition I'm afraid.

Well Todd, Mr Wafflebach said, pleased to meet ya. He shook my hand with some vigour and then sat down next to me, taking off his hat and producing a handkerchief to mop his brow. Hal had a brown rugged looking face. A face that looked like it had been there and done that. I surmised he would be about 60, from the grey stubble and salt and pepper moustache he sported. He ran his fingers through a thinning crop of hair.

Always this hot? He asked, sitting back on the bench and fanning himself with his hat.

Yes, most of the time, I answered.

Hot dog, Hal exclaimed. You visiting? I said I had been on business and was waiting for the Monday ferry. Hal digested the information then pointed to a woman walking towards us. She had an islander style dress, almost just a wrap around piece of cloth, with a pattern of frangipanis and a large straw coolie hat, which had been decorated with the local hibiscus. Her handbag dwarfed the ensemble. It was a woven palm frond thing that might fit a small child if you wanted to carry one, and was casually slung over her shoulder. She waved and padded over to our shady spot.

Wife, Hal said. Gloria this is Todd. We exchanged smiles and she plopped down on a dead palm log and took off her hat.

Pretty hot, she said in a southern drawl. Gloria had a shock of red hair that flew in all directions in varying degrees of curl She would never need a permanent, I thought. She ran her fingers through the nest and smiled.

Hal been bothering you Todd? I shook my head. She rummaged around in her bag and brought out two coca-cola drinks.

Sorry, I don't have another one, she apologised.

That's alright, I said as I watched Gloria take another dive into the bag and come up with a bottle opener. She popped the lids and Hal took his drink.

Should still be cold, Gloria said. They drank deeply and then Hal sighed.

Know these parts Todd? I told him I'd been up this way several times, but only for business.

What business? Hal asked. Americans I have met are very direct. They think nothing of asking you intimate details and are quick to reciprocate with their own.

I'm in the law, I said, not wanting to explain the intricacies of a travelling magistrate.

He's a lawyer, Hal said to his wife, who was once more diving into her bag.

Nice, Gloria answered, then continued to fossick.

And you? I asked Hal. I saw a smile creep across his face and knew he'd been waiting for this opening.

Treasure Hunter. The occupation was designed to intrigue. He sat forward wanting to go on and so I played the game.

Any luck?

Gloria popped her head up from her bag,

Tell Todd about the nugget Hal. It was all Hal needed to get going.

Klondike. Ever heard of it? Hal said.

Canada, I answered.

Hot dog that was a place. Gloria and I travelled up there by steamer, then train, then... Hal thought for a moment.

Hell, I can't remember, but it was a hard slog. You know it yielded 30 million in its day. 30 million Todd. They said it was finished. Hal tapped his nose. I knew better. Went there in the summer of '35 and you know I just about tripped over it. We were camped over by a ridge and I was walking out for the call of nature. Hal gave a chuckle. It was the darndest thing. I looked down and there it was.

Called the nugget Gloria. Hal looked at his wife and smiled.

32.17 troy ounces. That's just over 2.2 pounds. Kept us in boot polish for quite a while. Shaped like a Goddam peanut.

We sat still thinking on a nugget the shape of a peanut when Gloria brought out a pen and notebook and began to write. I looked on and Hal explained.

Gloria is a scribbler. Writes books and all that.

Oh, I said, what sort? I directed my question to Gloria.

Romance, she said.

Just a hobby isn't it Gloria? Hal said. She smiled at her husband.

Well, it keeps us in bread and butter. I'm Nora O'Neil. I frowned and wracked my brain. I had heard that name before.

Not *the* Nora O'Neil who...She didn't let me finish and completed my query.

Yes, that's me. Sold in just about every country that reads. Romance is popular.

This woman was a high flying author. I had read that her book sales outstripped the bible. She made herself comfortable and went to work. Hal brought me back to the nugget.

Texas man bought Gloria. Said he'd keep it intact. After that we went to Bolivia.

Bolivia? I said a little stunned.

Yep. Ancient pots. People pay a fortune for ancient pots. We had a bit of trouble with the Government, but it was sorted in the end. Turns out the president, Enrique Peñaranda reads romance. Isn't that right Gloria. Gloria nodded.

Then someone said they knew of a Chinese Emperor, buried in a boat on a goddam island off Japan. We bought the maps. Ever been to Japan Todd?

No, I said.

Little people. Short is what you'd call them. Bit touchy about digging up their land.

Did you find your Emperor? I said. Hal ruminated on my question then deftly changed the subject.

Did you know the Japanese read romance too. All those squiggles mean something. Gloria was a big hit over there, but it doesn't quite beat a gold nugget, does it cutey pie?

Gloria smiled at her husband.

So what brings you to Badu? I was intrigued. Hal came in close,

Pearls.

Pearls, I reiterated. Hal nodded.

Ever hear of a cyclone that came this way? On 4th March 1888, Mahina hit Bathurst Bay. Biggest storm and largest natural disaster in Australian history. Hot dog, they had thousands of sharks, fish and dolphins found several miles inland. Rocks embedded in trees. 125 mph winds and 400 dead. I listened as he continued.

Well know what else was lost that day? I shook my head. Pearling luggers. Lots of them. Now I know they weren't looking for pearls. They were in the business of shells, for buttons and stuff, but...Hal came in close again. There was one boat, the Nester. She was a trader going to South East Asia and she had a full load. He sat back and smirked. I reckon I know where she is.

And you can salvage these pearls? I asked.

Hot dog we can.

Won't it be an expensive exercise? Divers, boats, people in the know. Hal looked to his wife.

Gloria just got a Hollywood deal. They are paying good money, though it doesn't compare to gold nuggets. Isn't that right honey?

Gloria nodded and continued to write.

I tell her not to bust a gut with her scribbles. Why work for it when it's just there for the taking. We hit the big time in Klondike and who's to say it won't happen again. Easy money if you ask me.

I tried to fathom the relationship. Gloria seemed to be content to follow her husband's whims and fancies, just so long as she could write. It was obvious to me that she financed their lifestyle, although Hal couldn't see it.

So do you have everything lined up?

Well here's the thing Todd. How do you get these people to do anything? I want a boat. No problem they say and then no-one does anything about it. I need a diver. O.K. mister they say and then walk away. Hot dog, it ain't the way I do business. I smiled at his troubles.

On the islands everything is slow. That's just the way it is. Infuriating I know, but inevitable. Hal shook his head.

Hot dog, you hear that honey? Gloria looked up from her writing.

Hal honey, perhaps we should forget the pearls. Just put it in the too hard basket Hal. Hal thought on the proposition and then stuck his Stetson on his head.

Just going for a cold drink. He walked away and Gloria took his place on the seat.

What are you writing now? I asked.

It's a story of a pearling lugger, a boy and a girl. People like exotic locations. We looked at the aqua ocean lapping at the beach, the palm trees and colourful parrots squawking in the umbrella trees. I like to see these places and then I can write about them.

Hal returned with three coca-colas and had an expectant look in his eye.

Just been talking to the fellow in the shop. Says the army left all their vehicles behind. Imagine that. He sipped his drink. What do you think a jeep in worth these days? Or a truck?

I could see the wheels turning as he began to form a plan.

We could ship this stuff to.Fiji, or the Solomons. I bet they'd pay good money for a jeep. What do you say Snookums? Gloria shifted along on the bench and patted the spare spot for her husband to sit down.

It's not like finding a gold nugget, but I think it's a good idea Hal, she said.

Plate XVII

Bruno Cavello

Ingham, just off the coast of the Coral Sea is a little piece of Italy transported to North Queensland. There they eat pasta, work hard and have big families. I had come to Ingham on my way to the newly built Innisfail court house and had been stopped by heavy rains. I have always been partial to pasta and when the opportunity arises where I can have homemade authentic pasta, I take it. Caltibiano's cafe looked like a place where I could satisfy my hunger and I entered the small restaurant with about six tables and no customers.

The bell on the door announced my arrival and a short, round woman came out and pointed out the specials of the day. She had dark hair peppered with grey pulled back in a tight bun and hands that looked like they had done a lifetime of work. Gnarled and wrinkled, but capable and strong hands. She showed me to a table and then stood over me as I sat down to peruse my options. I opted for gnocchi, those small parcels of potato, with a creamy mushroom and spinach sauce. She applauded my choice and I complimented it with a glass of red wine. The wine was excellent, decanted from a small barrel and I guessed a house speciality. While I waited I admired the hand painted murals on the walls. I recognised the Roman Forum, the Colosseum, and a few other places when a gentleman came up and stood at my table.

You like? He said pointing to the pictures.

Yes, I said. They give the place a flavour of Italy.

My neighbour, he painted them. I am Lorenzo. He hitched up his trousers and said, This is my place. We smiled at one another. Lorenzo was a short stout man and matched the woman, who I guessed was his wife. He had a neat moustache and an unmistakable Roman nose and dark expressive eyes. His face was tanned and his brow furrowed with years of squinting into the sun, or worry, I imagined.

My neighbour, he is gone now.

Back to Italy? I asked. Lorenzo shook his head and put a course, meaty hand on my shoulder.

I will tell you about Bruno. He poured my glass of wine and leaned over to the adjacent table and grabbed another glass. He poured himself a generous amount then after a long sip he smiled at me, sat down and began.

Bruno Cavello, Lorenzo said, rolling the name around his mouth, was a cane cutter. He was strong, fit, young. The restaurateur patted his own belly. He didn't have the fat. He could cut all day and walk away at night with a whistle. A fine man was Bruno. From a little village outside Rome. He came to Australia to make good. It was like this for all of us. We come to make good. Lorenzo shot a glance to the kitchen where his wife was working.

I nodded and sipped my drink.

This was before the war. Before all the troubles. You want to be somebody then you have to go to America or Australia. There is no future in your village. Just old people and the mafioso.

Bruno came to the cane and he worked hard. It's easy when you are young. But when there is no cane to cut a man still has to live. So he paints, he fixes things and he builds things. Cupboards, beds, chairs. He is very good with making things. This goes on for a while and everyone knows Bruno as the man who can make you a new table, a stool, a crib. Still he cuts the cane every year. And he doesn't take a wife. Lorenzo looked to the kitchen again, and I thought I saw a level of familiarity in his eyes that only comes from years of marriage.

Sure, the women try to set him up, but he says no. He says he has other plans. Other plans. What could this be, we say. Everyone gets married. Then the children. It is natural. I have six. You married? Lorenzo asked me.

Yes, but my wife died a long time ago. He slapped his hand down on the table.

So you know this is the way. But Bruno, he was handsome. He was fit and he didn't look at the girls. We all begin to think he is twisted. Lorenzo cocked his little finger in the air and leaned on the table. You know?

Well, Bruno he just kept himself to himself. Then a few years ago I ask him to paint this for me. Lorenzo indicated the mural. Maria and I, we have a dream to make a restaurant. A little bit of home you know. He comes every day and works. It's a fine job. And when he works he is talking to me. We have a wine, we talk, he works, we feed him and he talks some more. And you know what he talks about?

I shook my head and raised an eyebrow.

Cloncurry.

Cloncurry?

That's right. He says he is finished with the cane and he is moving to Cloncurry. What is in Cloncurry I say. What do they have except flies, I say. But Bruno, he is set. He says he is selling up and going. No more cane for Bruno Cavello.

Lorenzo's wife appeared with my meal and after being served she stood over me while I tasted it. I made all the right noises and thanked her. Satisfied that she had excelled herself she left us to continue the story.

Eat, Lorenzo said. He pushed a basket of bread in my direction and I took a slice.

So, we say Bruno must be mad. He must be thinking of somewhere else.

You ever been to Cloncurry?

I nodded while chewing.

You like it?

I shrugged my shoulders not wanting to talk with a mouthful of the most delicious gnocchi I had ever tasted.

So we all look at the map. Out in
nowhere is Cloncurry. So we try to talk
It's no place for a man like Bruno. All th
ugly, we say. There are no Italian baker
But you can't change a man's mind with w
is set. Bruno Cavello was set.

So he finished the wall and I say, w
other wall, you know, trying to keep him
but he says no. He says he is busy. He say
We watch as he sells his things. Car, hou
everything. What will you sit on, we say.
travel around, we ask. But Bruno says he
Then one day he is gone. Lorenzo clicked
Just like that.

We refilled out wine glasses and I tucked into
my dinner.

So, after a while we forget Bruno. You know,
life is like that. People now and again see the painting
and say,

Where is Bruno, but he is gone and life goes on.
Then one day, Lorenzo put down his glass and lent his
elbows on the table, someone comes from Cloncurry
and says they have seen a strange thing. It is a joke they
say. It is a boat being built in a back yard in Cloncurry.
A sailing boat.

Well...this is a good story and we all say,
imagine that. A boat being built in a back yard 500
miles from the sea. The man says he has seen it with his
own eyes. This man says it is a fine boat. The man who
builds this boat knows what he is doing. He is Italian.
Well, we can all see what is right in front of us. Bruno
Cavello has gone mad. Completely pazzo, crazy.

We feel he is family and so we decide that someone needs to go and see for themselves.

And you were elected to go? I asked putting down my fork.

Me. Lorenzo Caltibiano. Lorenzo sat back as we digested the information.

I have a car and I drove all the way to Cloncurry. Maria can look after the restaurant. We say it is our duty to look after Bruno. He is like family. Lorenzo picked at a piece of bread and dunked it in his wine then ate.

There is nothing but dirt from here to Cloncurry. No green. Nothing. He refilled my glass and his own and we drank.

So, I make it to Cloncurry in three days. He held up three stubby fingers. My car isn't very fast, but reliable. And what do you think I find when I arrive? Eveyone knows of the crazy Italian who is building a boat. They ask me if I am coming to help sail it away. It is all a big joke, this Italian mad man. So I go to find Bruno. It's not hard. First you see the mast above the houses and then when you turn the corner you can see the boat. It is a fine example. A beautiful yacht with long lines. A wooden masterpiece. Lorenzo smacked his fingers to his lips. 56 feet. Planked and painted white and blue.

I'd imagine he was surprised to see you, I said.

You bet. He was up a ladder on this yacht and I called out, hey Cavello and Bruno just about fell off the ladder. We are like family to him, the Caltibianos and the Cavellos. Lorenzo crossed his two fingers to accentuate the point. Well we have a fine time drinking wine and talking of Ingham and all the people we know, but all the time I can't get the words out. Can't say what I want to say. It is like I have swallowed a ravioli as big as a book. I want to say he must come home. I want to tell him people think he is crazy and I want to let him know we care about him, but all these words are stuck. Lorenzo took a long draft of his wine and then called his wife for more.

She came in and seeing my plate empty cleared away then fetched the wine.

Bruno I can see is happy. He is fit and healthy and he has the look of a man who is content. Why should I say anything I ask myself? He is doing nothing wrong. The man is doing what he wants to do and that is a rare thing. Lorenzo looked at his wife fussing in the kitchen. So I said nothing. He showed me his boat. It was a beautiful thing. Bruno says to me he is making plans. He says to me he is getting ready. I'm not sure what he means, but after the wine I don't care. I stayed overnight in Cloncurry. Bruno says I can stay with him and so we drink, we talk and we parted as cousins.

When I come back to Ingham I have to explain all this to our friends. They want to know all the details and all we can talk about for days is Bruno Cavello. Some still call him mad, but a man who is happy doing what he wants...this is not mad, this is a man who has everything.

I nodded in agreement as the wine slipped down my throat making me relaxed and less inclined to talk and more inclined to listen.

So life goes on and Bruno is forgotten. Cloncurry is a long way away and the cane grows for another season and another and nothing much else matters until we have a cyclone.

She is a beauty. Category 4 they say. A real storm. The rain goes for days, weeks and the rivers flood. It is a terrible time for us. The cane is strong, but this storm takes it from the earth and throws it flat, trampled by the foot of God.

And then we hear that the storm is making trouble inland. Towns cut off, rivers raging. It is a wild time.

Have you been in a cyclone? Lorenzo asked.

No, I try not to travel in the summer season. I have seen the floods. It is a terrifying sight to see the Burdekin in full flood. Lorenzo poured himself another glass of wine and I finished the second bottle.

After the storm there is the cleaning up. Trees everywhere, roads washed away, houses shattered. But we are ok here. The water came to here, Lorenzo pointed to the Colosseum on the painting. Ingham is sore, but not beaten. Well I was cleaning up when I began to think of Bruno. How would he be in the middle of nowhere, but there is work to do and so I just forget him.

It was around two months after that a man came into my restaurant and he says he has heard something strange. A man in a yacht sailed out of Cloncurry and just disappeared. Imagine that. Lorenzo clapped his hands on the table. Just disappeared. It must be Bruno we say to this man. There is a river we say. Bruno is sailing to the sea we are sure.

Then the next cane season comes and goes and we begin to hear stories. A yacht has been seen in

Charters Towers. A boat is said to be in Mt Isa. It can only be Bruno.

Over the seasons we hear less and less then one day a bloke comes in from Camooweal. He swears he has seen a yacht there in the middle of nowhere. He thinks he is crazy with the heat and the flies, but he can see a boat. It must be Bruno. Have you been to Camooweal?

Yes.

Anything there?

Nothing but the pub and a few hardy souls, I said.

You reckon a boat could get there.

I pondered the question. I had seen and heard too many stories of the bush to discount anything.

Maybe, I said.

Maybe, Lorenzo repeated and drained his wine glass. Maybe it is true, but a man doing what he wants to do, that is the real story.

PLATES: I ~ XVII

(I) Trododniak Weatherness
Jas Christie, Mayor of Mackay 1910 - 1911.
Image sourced for Picture Queensland, State Library of Queensland.
John Oxley Library image number 15057
http://hdl.handle.net/10462/deriv/60754

(II) Archer Frankston
Trainee soldiers at Roma Street station, Brisbane waiting to embark to Caloundra.
Image sourced for Picture Queensland, State Library of Queensland.
John Oxley library neg number 73715
http://hdl.handle.net/10462/deriv/69377

(III) Rufus Mcfadden
Coopers Garage in Moreton Street, Eidesvold, 1930.
Image sourced for Picture Queensland, State Library of Queensland.
John Oxley Library Negative number: 180653
http://hdl.handle.net/10462/deriv/98272

(IV) Erik Van Bootman
Panoramic View of Gladstone 1937-38.
Image sourced for Picture Queensland, State Library of Queensland.
John Oxley Library Image number: APE-078-0001-0031
http://hdl.handle.net/10462/deriv/124269

(V) Boy
Hotel Magee, Collinsville.
Kind permission of Julia Duncan, granddaughter of Annie Duncan, owner the Hotel Magee during the 1930s - 40s.

(VI) Martin Swineburne
Queensland National Bank, Julia Creek 1940.
Image sourced for Picture Queensland, State Library of Queensland.
John Oxley Library, number 203194
http://hdl.handle.net/10462/deriv/201979

(VII) Lionel Arkwright
menswear for sale in V. Hellen's store, Goomeri, 1940.
Image sourced for Picture Queensland, State Library of Queensland.
John Oxley Library Negative number: 101740
http://hdl.handle.net/10462/deriv/92006

(VIII) Seymour Ham
Elsanna, supply ship to Thursday Island.
Image sourced for Picture Queensland, State Library of Queensland.
John Oxley Library Negative number: 30060
http://hdl.handle.net/10462/deriv/89205

(IX) Miss Willmott and Mr Crick Albert Barrett & Friend
Magnetic Hotel at Picnic Bay, Townsville.
Image sourced for Picture Queensland, State Library of Queensland.
John Oxley Library Negative number: 99243
http://hdl.handle.net/10462/deriv/78683

(X) Edward Addison
Oak Street, Barcaldine.
Image sourced for Picture Queensland, State Library of Queensland.
John Oxley Library Negative number: 201142
http://hdl.handle.net/10462/deriv/117630

(XI) Dolly & Harold Lancome
Ships loading at Eagle Street Wharf, Brisbane.
Image sourced for Picture Queensland, State Library of Queensland.
John Oxley Library Negative number: 167716
http://hdl.handle.net/10462/deriv/135110

(XII) Flora Rhinehart
Post Office Hotel, Camooweal 1953.
Image sourced for Picture Queensland, State Library of Queensland.
John Oxley Library Negative number: 128605
http://hdl.handle.net/10462/deriv/81944

(XIII) Pat
C.W.A. Hall in Winton circa 1940.
Image sourced for Picture Queensland, State Library of Queensland.
John Oxley Library Negative number: 74461
http://hdl.handle.net/10462/deriv/67617

(XIV) Albert Barrett & Friend
Tolano's Excelsior Hotel, Charters Towers.
Image sourced for Picture Queensland, State Library of Queensland.
John Oxley Library Negative number: 129737
http://hdl.handle.net/10462/deriv/83051

(XV) Lola & Reverend Stanley Pinks
Methodist Church and manse in Cooktown 1940.
Image sourced for Picture Queensland, State Library of Queensland.
John Oxley Library Negative number: 31724
http://hdl.handle.net/10462/deriv/84952

(XVI) Hal & Gloria Wafflebach
Pearling Luggers leaving Thursday Island, Torres Straits.
Image sourced for Picture Queensland, State Library of Queensland.
John Oxley Library Image number: APO-032-0001-0020
http://hdl.handle.net/10462/deriv/38459

(XVII) Bruno Cavello
Sugar cane worker carrying a bundle of cut cane at Nambour, Queensland, 1938.
Image sourced for Picture Queensland, State Library of Queensland.
John Oxley Library Negative number: 71785
http://hdl.handle.net/10462/deriv/69786

Made in the USA
Columbia, SC
06 November 2017